# Alpha Eternal

by

Brenda Sparks

*Alpha Council Chronicles, Book 6*

**Alpha Eternal**


Contact Information: info@thewildrosepress.com

Cover Art by *Rae Monet, Inc. Designs*

The Wild Rose Press, Inc.
PO Box 708
Adams Basin, NY 14410-0708
Visit us at www.thewildrosepress.com

Publishing History
First Black Rose Edition, 2020
Trade Paperback ISBN 978-1-5092-3433-2
Digital ISBN 978-1-5092-3434-9

*Alpha Council Chronicles, Book 6*
Published in the United States of America

"So, what brings you here, Shira?" *As if I didn't know.*

"I was told to keep…I-I just wondered where you were."

*Told to keep an eye on me is more likely.* Why else would she have stuck to him like glue every second he'd been here? He really shouldn't complain. As guards went, she was a good-looking one, even if she needed an attitude adjustment now and then.

"Well, you found me."

"Yeah, after searching around for hours. Why aren't you in the communications room working on the computers?"

He shrugged. "I can't do anything more until we figure out a way to cool the room, so the server won't overheat."

"Then shouldn't you be thinking about that instead of messing about down here in the garage?" Shira accused hotly.

"I'll have you know I do my best thinking under a car." Perspiration trickled down his chest. Hunger flashed in Shira's eyes as they followed the trail. Damn, it was fun getting her all riled up.

"And have you come up with a solution?" Shira moved a little closer as if she was afraid to get too near.

"I might have. Give me a little while longer to reason it through." He grabbed two bottles of water from the top of the toolbox. "Want a drink?"

Shira took the one he offered. He tipped the other to his mouth and drained it in long swallows, allowing her a lengthy stare at him standing there half naked, head tipped back. Alex heard a soft moan push through her lips and struggled not to smile around the bottle.

## Praise for Brenda Sparks

"Brenda Sparks weaves stories that are filled with sensuality, mystery, drama, and awesome vampire action. They keep you on the edge of your seat and never fail to deliver a satisfying conclusion."

*~Author DW Adler*

~*~

"Ms. Sparks takes you on a journey that'll have you turning pages just to find out what happens."

*~Author Rhea Regale*

**Dedication**

This final story in the Alpha Council Chronicles series
is dedicated with many thanks to YOU, the fans.
I'll always be thankful for your support of the Alphas.
This has been a marvelous and exciting journey.
I hope you love this last tale as much as you love
the Alphas themselves.
As Alex would say,
I hope y'all enjoyed the ride, my darlin's.

**Acknowledgments**

Much gratitude goes to my heartmate; I couldn't write without his love and support.

Of course, I'll always be thankful to my family and friends for their encouragement.

And last but most certainly not least, I owe sincere gratitude to my amazing editor, Callie Lynn Wolfe, cover artist Rae Monet, and the wonderful staff at The Wild Rose Press for helping me share the Alpha Council Chronicles series with the world.

A HUGE thank-you to everyone who believed in me and helped my dreams come true.

# Chapter 1

"That is one dumb-ass plan, Stephan!" Malice dripped from Tatiana's voice when she turned and faced the leader of the Alpha Council.

"Tatiana," Demetri admonished softly, though every vampire in the room heard the castigation.

When the female warrior rounded on her mate, the daggers which shot from her eyes would have been enough to quell most males. As the only female on the Alpha Council, their leader, Stephan, granted her a certain amount of leeway. However, the look of censure on his face matched the tone in her mate's voice.

Their leader rose from the couch, pulled at the sleeves of his black turtleneck shirt, then lowered his arms to his sides. Stephan's stance appeared open, legs shoulder-width apart, hands relaxed by his thighs, but his presence projected a deadly menace. His dark blue eyes narrowed on Tatiana.

Demetri immediately rose, placing himself between Stephan and his mate. Instead of addressing the threat, he turned and rested a meaty hand on her shoulder.

Alex stared in awe at the scene. No one challenged Stephan. No. One. And yet this skinny woman with the personality of a tiger challenged him openly in front of the entire Council.

They had all gathered at Nicholai's mansion to

discuss Stephan's plan for dealing with the latest big baddy. That was their mission, after all, to take out the worst of the worst, and boy, they recently discovered the worst.

The sire of one of their members had worked with a group of devious demons to resurrect The Source, an ancient vampire whose powers seemed unlimited, and to date, they'd been unable to discover any weaknesses. It was for that reason Stephan made a proposal for demons and vampires to join together to take down The Source—a proposal Tatiana strongly disagreed with and obviously had no qualms about sharing her disapproval with the group.

Alex pushed a hand through his blond hair. He didn't understand why Tatiana was so up in arms; it was his ass being sent into the fire.

Pulling Alex from his reverie, Demetri said, "I realize you disapprove of the exchange between our breeds, but I trust Stephan. He would never suggest such a thing without a good reason."

Tatiana's yellow, cat-like eyes softened. "I hate them for what they did to you, Demetri."

Demetri wrapped his arms around her leather clad body and pulled her against his chest. He rested his chin on top of her black hair. "I know you do, *kotik kisa.* But I survived their torture. I am here with you, whole once more. And while I'll never trust them, I do trust Stephan. If he thinks this is the best way for us to defeat the one the demons call The Source, then I defer to his wisdom. Stephan has never let me down in the hundreds of years we have fought together. Trust in him. Trust in me."

"Of course, I trust you, Demetri." Tatiana wrapped

her arms around his thick waist.

Demetri had spent hundreds of years on his own. Hadn't needed anyone. Had been a thorn in their sides for as long as Alex could remember. But finding his heartmate changed all of that. Changed him. Okay, so he was still a sonofabitch, but he was now an utterly devoted, softer around the edges, somewhat cooperative, sonofabitch. It almost made a guy want to find a heartmate.

"Tatiana," Stephan spoke, drawing everyone's attention. "I understand your feelings. Quite honestly, I share them in regard to the demons. I'd like nothing more than to kill the ones who have hurt our people with my bare hands. But there is a bigger threat out there. Eldrick is the most powerful being I have ever come across, and the demons have information about him we need. I don't trust the demons any more than you or Demetri do. However, I see no alternative to working with them for now. At least until we bring down Eldrick.

"To that end, I have arranged with the king of the demons for Alex to go and stay for a while in the demon compound."

Stephan pinned Alex with his intense gaze. "I trust you will be able to infiltrate them, find the information we need to take out Eldrick."

Alex nodded. "Of course."

If only he felt as confident as he sounded. He was going into the demonic compound under the guise of setting up a communication system to make it easier for them and the vampires to share information and coordinate efforts. In reality, Stephan charged him with finding out all they knew about vampires and Eldrick.

According to Nicholai, he'd seen firsthand that the demons possessed the ability to bring someone back from the brink of death. A demon named Harleigh did just that for Nicholai's sister, Natasha. And Stephan wanted to learn what other abilities and secrets the demons possessed.

"Don't worry, Stephan. I will discover all I can about the demonic breed and report it back to you."

Nicholai crossed one leg, resting his ankle on the opposite knee. "I understand why you want Alex to go spy on the demons, but I cannot fathom why you would allow a demon to remain with us."

"Varrick requested an exchange. It was the only way he'd allow Alex within his walls." Stephan shifted his weight to his other foot.

Desmond pushed away from the wall. "Plus, Harleigh won't be any trouble. After all, she and Natasha are friends."

His proper British accent made him sound like he'd stepped out of Buckingham Palace. For a moment, Alex wished he spoke with that accent instead of his Virginian twang, then he quickly decided he'd rather not sound so uppity.

A baby's cry turned Vlad's head in the direction of the door.

"Does the child need you, Vlad?"

"No. Natasha said nothing is wrong, he is simply hungry." Vlad settled back into his chair, appearing stressed. The tiny lines etched around his eyes, and the dark circles gave him a menacing look. He scrubbed a hand over his black goatee before sending it over his shaved head.

*Being a new dad must be making him wary*, Alex

decided. *Probably the lack of sleep mixed with the threat Eldrick represented doesn't help.*

Of course, with a baby in the house and preternatural hearing, none of them were getting much sleep these days. It would almost be a vacation to go live with the demons for a while.

*Yeah, right!* Alex rolled his eyes.

Marcus shifted forward, resting his forearms on his thighs. "Since Harleigh is already here, when does Alex leave for the demon compound?"

"Tonight," Stephan replied.

"Tonight?" Alex's brows shot up and touched his blond bangs. "How am I supposed to get there? I can't dematerialize there. I don't know where it is."

Stephan gave him a small grin. "I thought of that. Turns out Varrick's compound is near Demetri's home in Wyoming. Varrick said he would send someone to Demetri's house to escort you to the compound."

"They know where Demetri lives?" Marcus asked.

"They kidnapped me from there." Demetri reminded the young Alpha.

Hate flashed in Tatiana's eyes. "I'll kill them."

"Sonofabitch," Marcus muttered.

"The only demons you will kill, Tatiana, are the ones assisting Eldrick."

"Jara," Demetri supplied the name of the demon not only helping Eldrick but who had been instrumental in Demetri's torture as well.

"That bitch is mine." Tatiana's gaze swept the room as if she dared anyone to deny her the kill.

Stephan held up his hands. "We'll deal with her when we find her. But to find her, we'll need information and probably the help of her kind. Which is why I didn't want to waste one more night getting Alex into the compound. The sooner he gets there, the sooner he can get us the information we need."

*Annnnd* didn't that just make his night. No time like the present as the saying went.

"You ready to go, Alex?" Stephan asked.

"Just need to pop home first and grab some clothes…and of course, blood to take with me."

"I can give you the address to the local blood bank and hospital where you can get more when needed," offered Demetri.

Alex nodded. "Thanks, man."

"What are the rest of us going to do, while Alex is off playing James Bond?" Marcus asked his sire, Stephan.

"I thought it best we remain together."

"You are all welcome to stay in my home," offered Nicholai.

Stephan grinned. "Thank you, my old friend, for the gracious offer, but I have another place in mind. We must train, sharpen our skills before we take on Eldrick again. I thought perhaps Marcus' home might be best, since he has more than enough rooms for all of us, and he recently built the training center out back."

"Christina and I would be happy to put your sorry asses up at our place." Marcus smiled and leaned back in his seat.

Alex agreed it made sense. Marcus' plantation in Savannah would easily accommodate the rest of the Alphas and their mates. With a full gym, pool, and an automated state-of-the-art training center, it would provide the perfect place for the Alphas to train while keeping their mates safe.

Stephan's grin reached his eyes. "Thank you. When I saved your life on that battlefield, I figured you'd come in handy one day. Just wish it hadn't taken over two hundred years for you to finally be of use."

Marcus growled in mock anger, then chuckled. "Yeah, yeah, yeah. Like I've never saved your ass before."

"Language, Marcus," Demetri growled. "There is a lady present."

Tatiana hauled off and hit him in the shoulder hard enough he staggered.

While Demetri rubbed his shoulder, Stephan cleared his throat to garner everyone's attention. "So, we are clear. Alex will materialize to Demetri's place in Wyoming tonight, while we make our way to Marcus' plantation. Since the baby and Nicholai's heartmate can't dematerialize, I'll have my private plane take Juliette, Harleigh, Natasha, and baby Viktor to Savannah."

"I would like to accompany my mate on the plane," Nicholai stated.

"As would I," Vlad concurred.

"Of course," Stephan agreed.

"I'd be willing to go on your plane as well," Desmond offered.

Everyone turned a questioning cye on the relatively new member of the team. "You know where Marcus' house is and can materialize there. Why would you wish to go on the plane?"

Silence met Stephan's question. Alex thought it was a rather good inquiry. He understood why the other two warriors would want to fly with their mates. But for Desmond to choose hours on a plane rather than seconds, well that made no sense.

Before the question could be answered, a knock sounded on the door.

"Come in," Stephan called out.

A tiny woman pushed through the door. Her elfin features, small nose, and predominate cheekbones made her violet eyes all the more striking. Apparently, Desmond must have thought so as well, because he straightened a little when she entered the room.

Harleigh tossed her multi-colored hair off her shoulders before she spoke. Every day her hair had been a different color. She changed it more often than her shoes, and, according to Natasha, it was because the demon could shapeshift. Apparently, she had the ability to shift the locks into any color-or combination of colors-she wanted.

Harleigh was pretty enough, he guessed, but nothing compared to Juliette's sister, the supermodel. Now there was a real beauty. Holy Hell, that Samantha was hotter than a radiator on a race car. She really got his engine revving. He hadn't seen her since Nicholai and Julie's wedding, but he hoped to rectify that soon. At least she'd given him her number. With all his fellow Alphas finding their mates lately, he began to see the benefits of settling down.

"Natasha informed me of your plan." Harleigh put her fisted hands on her hips. "Don't you think you might have asked me first if I minded being hauled off to the States?"

Her thick Australian accent made her sound like she'd just stepped out of the Outback.

Stephan moved across the room in three powerful strides to stand in front of her. "I assumed since Varrick requested you remain with us, as an ambassador of sorts, you would accompany us to Savannah."

She crossed her arms over her chest and glared up at him. "It still would have been nice of you to ask. Perhaps I don't want to go to Savannah. Maybe I have a fear of flying."

Stephan raised one eyebrow. "Do you?"

"Well, no, but still you might have asked."

"Is there a reason why you cannot join us in Savannah, instead of here?"

The demon's eyes softened. "Well, no, but—"

"Then it is settled," Stephan announced. "Go pack. The plane will be here shortly."

"But I—" Desmond's hand wrapping around her arm cut Harleigh's statement short.

Alex did not miss the shudder that went through her body when Desmond spoke. "Let's go, Harleigh. I'll help you pack."

"You most certainly will not," the tiny demon protested while DW led her from the room by the arm. "I can do it myself."

Watching the two of them together, Alex suddenly realized why Desmond wanted to go on the plane—Harleigh. He worked to keep the knowing smile from his face. A demon and a vampire, yeah like that would ever work. Give him a human any day, preferably a sexy supermodel type of human. There just happened to be a little something he needed to take care of first.

"We finished here, boss?" Alex asked Stephan.

"I believe so."

"Then I'm going to take off. The sooner I get to Wyoming, the sooner I can get the intel and bug outta there."

Stephan moved closer and clamped a large hand down hard on Alex's shoulder. "I appreciate your sacrifice. It will not be easy living amongst the demons, and I'm not sure how long you'll be with them."

Anticipation knotted his belly, but he swallowed the trepidation. If the team needed him, he'd do his duty. For he was the kind of guy who rose to the occasion—even when the occasion called for living with a breed of beings he didn't trust any further than he could throw a building.

He sighed deeply. It was time to meet his destiny. And he'd meet it as he met every challenge—head on.

## Chapter 2

Varrick watched the water flow over a section of the rock wall and cascade over his mate as she stood in the bath. The large bathroom, with its smooth, polished stone walls and floors, matched those of the anteroom—matched the entire compound.

Tucked inside the Wyoming mountain, the fortress had been carved in the rock. The surrounding detritus kept his home at a perfect sixty-five degrees year-round. An underground spring provided not only water to drink, but places where it had broken through the granite, provided natural showers that ran all day long at a warm seventy-seven degrees.

The demon king leaned back on the granite vanity and observed Elizabeth lather her hair. The soapy suds sluiced over her flesh. His eyes traced their slippery trail. Bubbles rolled over her taught stomach and thin hips to caress the lion tattoo on her left thigh then the vine of ivy that snaked around her right ankle and foot.

She turned in the water and rinsed the suds from her golden hair, presenting her backside. His gaze immediately fell to the pattern tattooed on the small of her back. When they'd first met, she'd called it a tribal tramp stamp, but he knew otherwise for it was the ancient demonic symbol for ruler. And prior to making his acquaintance, she'd placed it on her body, like a sign for him.

As his mate, she ruled by his side, providing a calming presence his savage heart needed. And if ever there was a time he needed calming, it was now. Varrick closed his eyes, and a heavy sigh pushed through his lips.

"What is it?" Elizabeth asked.

"Just thinking."

The king opened his eyes as she stepped from the shower.

Elizabeth wrapped a towel around her tiny four-foot eleven-inch frame. Varrick grabbed a towel and patted her long hair. He wrapped the golden strands in the brown terry cloth and rubbed them.

Their eyes met in the mirror when she spoke. "Thinking about the vampires?"

"What else?" He massaged the towel over her scalp. "I hope I have done the right thing."

She turned, put her arms around his waist, and gazed up into his eyes. "You did what you thought was right, you always do."

Varrick dropped the towel and brought their bodies together in a tight hug. He could get lost in her. The sensation of her soft skin pressed against his made his most impressive part twitch, but they didn't have time to take care of it the way he'd like. A member of the Alpha Council was on the way, and they needed to be ready to receive him.

"I wish you were right, Elizabeth. Wish all my decisions were perfect, but alas, I've made mistakes, and our people suffered the consequences."

Her arms tightened around him before she laid her cheek against his chest. "Don't, Varrick. Don't sell yourself short. You always do what you believe to be necessary."

"And look what it cost us. My people are still vulnerable to human diseases, even though I authorized experimentation on the vampires to find a cure. One of the top scientific minds of our kind is dead because I allowed my sister to oversee the experiments. My own sister released The Source upon the world and has been kidnapped or worse, may be working with the creature. We don't know what they have planned, but it can't be good, and all of these things are ultimately my doing."

Elizabeth's eyes softened before she sighed. "I see things differently. Your people die from the simple common cold because their immune systems are not strong. Just like anyone else, you tried to find a cure."

"But the cure led to vampires."

"I'm not condoning the kidnapping, but until Cyrus told you what happened to the vampires who were taken, you had no idea Lane was being so cruel with his experiments."

Worry creased his forehead. "I authorized the experimentation. I should have kept a closer eye on things."

Her hand stroked his back. "You sent your sister, Jara, to do that, trusting she'd do as you would have done."

"And look how well that decision worked out. She accidentally killed Lane in a fit of anger, sent Leo to steal a tome from this very fortress, and is now with the most powerful being I've ever encountered."

"Varrick, what exactly happened with The Source?"

He tucked his mate under his arm and led her into their room. As they parted, he allowed his energy to coalesce in the palm of his hand. When it grew to the size of a softball and glowed a healthy white-hot, he tossed it into the granite hearth. The kindling within caught ablaze. Now it would be warm while Elizabeth dressed.

Shadows danced over Elizabeth's beautiful face from the glow of the flames. Highlights glistened in her hair. She appeared striking, and Varrick wondered what he'd done to deserve her.

"The Source?" she prompted, then settled onto the overstuffed golden couch. "You've stalled long enough. You promised to tell me."

He sat beside her and stared into the mesmerizing fire, listening to it crackle. "I don't have much to tell. Presumably, the tome Jara's lackey stole contained information on The Source."

"What is The Source?"

Varrick laid an arm on the back of the couch. "A legend from my childhood. A phantom our parents told us about to scare us. I never thought they'd based the story in truth."

He shook his head and rubbed a thick hand over his perpetually stubbled jaw. Memories of his parents flowed through his mind, bringing a shudder to his body.

"It is said The Source is a being of unlimited power who stalked the earth destroying everyone he encountered. He drained his victims' blood, ate them whole, raped and pillaged entire villages. With no weaknesses, no way to destroy him, our ancestors did the next best thing, they put him in a permanent stasis and hid him from the world."

"Why would Jara seek out such a beast?"

"I couldn't begin to guess. Perhaps she thought she'd found a way to kill him…perhaps she thought to create an alliance with him to rule the world. I put nothing past her. She is not the sister I grew up with."

Elizabeth snuggled against his chest, resting an arm around his stomach. The warmth soaked into his flesh through his dress shirt. Her touch calmed him, brought peace and a sense of tranquility. Muscles he hadn't realized were bunched relaxed.

"I'm sorry, Varrick. I know you love her."

"*Loved* her," he corrected. "I loved the sister I knew in childhood. The woman Jara has become is not anyone I can love. She is a stranger to me, a threat to our people. She must be dealt with. And now that she has resurrected The Source…if she joined forces with him, she will be a force to be reckoned with."

"But you have the vampires to help."

He ran his hand down Elizabeth's damp hair. "It is a tenuous alliance at best, Little Bits. The vampires do not trust me any more than I trust them."

"But you are allowing one to stay with us."

"I only agreed to that because I believe we need the help of the Alpha Council to take down The Source. It was Stephan's idea for the one called Alexander to come here and supposedly set up a communication system."

"Supposedly? So, you think the vampire has another mission here?"

*Smart woman.* She never missed a thing. "I cannot trust a bloodsucker, Elizabeth. They are secretive creatures by nature. Do I believe Stephan when he said we needed to work together? Yes. Do we need to be able to communicate with one another to do that? Yes.

Do I think this Alexander will help make it happen? Perhaps, but our location in this mountain has always made things difficult, especially using technology."

"So, you don't believe the vampire will be able to set up phone service or the internet?"

Varrick noticed the tone of her voice.

"Don't despair, little one." He kissed the top of her head. "I know you are hoping to access the internet again. I realize you have missed it since moving here from Mason's Bluff. I am sorry for all you have given up to be with me."

Elizabeth pushed away and looked directly into his eyes. "I love you, Varrick. I do not regret my decision to come live here with you. There is nowhere I'd rather be. I've not given anything up. Instead, I've gained much by loving you."

Hearing the declaration lightened his mood. Hope filled his heart. "I hope Alexander will live up to Stephan's hype. But, just in case, I have assigned Caden to escort him while on the premises."

"Caden, your second in command? Won't he be intimidating?"

"That is the point. I want to be sure the vampire knows I do not trust him."

A thoughtful look graced her face. "But don't you think knowing he is being watched will keep him from doing anything underhanded? Perhaps you should consider assigning someone less threatening. Someone he can be at ease around."

"Like whom?"

Elizabeth tugged her lower lip between her teeth as she paused to ponder his question. The sight sent lust zinging through his blood.

"A woman," she finally said. "He'll underestimate a woman, believe her inferior, not see her as a threat. He'll be more likely to let his guard down."

"So, if he has a hidden agenda, she might discover what it is."

"Exactly." A smug smile took her full lips.

"You are brilliant," Varrick exclaimed, eyeing her tempting mouth.

He leaned forward and brushed his lips against hers. An electric jolt traveled straight to his groin, making it tingle. His large hand cupped her cheek, and he deepened the kiss. Great Spirits, she made him react like a schoolboy, made him hard with only a look.

Elizabeth moaned, the sound soft and sensual. He swallowed it, taking it into his soul. He broke the caress, feathering kisses along the line of her jaw, down her throat. She tasted of fresh spring water and woman. His inner beast roared in anticipation of mating. His body tightened with desire.

"Varrick?" Her breathy whisper registered in his ears.

"What, little one?" he spoke against her neck. He relished the shiver that went through her when his hot breath ghosted over her skin. Goosebumps pebbled her delicate flesh.

"We don't have time for this."

"We always have time for this." He nibbled on the soft spot where her neck met her shoulder.

"But the vampire…"

Her thoughts were of another male, *a vampire,* now? Varrick pulled away, pinning her with his hard stare. "What about him?"

"He should be here soon."

"So?" Varrick rose one eyebrow.

"So, we need to get ready to receive him."

"Worried we'll keep him waiting, my sweet?" Varrick returned to her neck, placing an invisible necklace of kisses around.

"I sent Cyrus and Caden to retrieve him." His tongue darted out to lave over the goose pimples covering her skin. "And I don't care if we keep him waiting."

"I—"

Her sentence ended when he took her lips in a demanding kiss and pulled the towel from her body.

****

Alex materialized in front of Demetri's Wyoming home with a duffle bag full of clothes in one hand and a cooler of blood in the other. He glanced down at his watch, noting he arrived exactly at the time he indicated he would meet the demons.

His eyes scanned the surrounding area. The pines, with their thick green foliage, contrasted against the bare branches of the other trees and bushes. It was November, and the temperature had dropped, making winter come early to the forest. He paced back and forth, boots crunching on the leaf-covered ground.

Alex's preternatural sense of smell informed him he was not alone in these woods. Small creatures were nearby along with a bear and…

He sent his awareness flowing over the land. It confirmed the animals, but it also told him much more. He sensed two blanks.

*Demons.*

They moved his way, on less than silent feet. His acute hearing easily picked up their traipsing through the forest.

His body tensed when they rounded the corner of Demetri's home. Varrick had sent two large males. The larger of the two wore his hair shaved close to his head. His intense stare narrowed on Alex. Thanks to his vampiric vision he clearly made out details on the male through the pitch of the night.

The male boasted a warrior's build. Thick neck and arms, broad shoulders. Slightly taller than Demetri and every bit as wide, the male's red eyes reflected menace and disdain.

The male with him carried himself with confidence and a slight arrogance. Shaggy blond hair fell into his eyes. He stood a little shorter than Alex, about two inches, and while fit, he wasn't muscular.

"Hello, boys," Alex greeted with a nod of his head. "I take it you are my escorts for this evenin'."

The larger one spoke first. "You are the one called Alexander?"

"Yes. But call me Alex." The Alpha hoped being informal might put them at ease.

"Follow me," the large one commanded, and the pair turned their backs.

*Guess not*, Alex thought wryly and wondered what their names were. *Apparently, their mamas didn't teach them any manners.*

The trio walked in uncomfortable silence through the forest until Alex couldn't take it any longer. "What are your names, if you don't mind me asking?"

"I'm Cyrus," the blond responded. "And he is Caden."

"Nice to meet you." Alex wasn't surprised when Caden simply grunted in response.

Not exactly friendly types, but then he wasn't here to make friends, so it really didn't matter.

After twenty chilly minutes, they came upon a mountain. Alex's gaze followed the rock face as a chunk of it slid open. Inside, a long tunnel carved from the rock was lit by torches held in sconces on the walls.

Alex followed the demons inside, and the rock slid closed while they marched down the hall.

He glanced behind them but didn't see how the opening worked. No mechanisms were visible, no pulleys, no hinges. The impressive engineering made Alex's mechanical mind long to discover how exactly it worked, but the demons gave him no time to take in the marvel. They marched down the hall at a brisk clip, leaving Alex little choice but to follow.

The rock walls were not as smooth as the floor which made for very interesting shadow play from the torches as they moved past one wooden door after another.

Caden pushed through a set of double doors, and Alex barely contained his gasp. His eyes swept the room. The granite walls curved from floor into ceiling, which in turn curved down to form regularly spaced columns. In the middle of the room, a three-tiered fountain flowed. Fire poured over the tiers and pooled in the large basin, sending yellow and orange light around the room, illuminating the polished walls.

At the end of the cavernous room, two thrones with velvet padding sat on a rock dais.

"Wait here," Caden commanded. He left the room, closing Alex and Cyrus in.

Alex placed his bag and cooler on the floor. "So, what is this place?"

"The Receiving Room."

"Who is going to receive me?"

"King Varrick and Elizabeth."

"I know who Varrick is, but who is Elizabeth?"

The demon shifted as if uncomfortable answering the question. "She is the queen of the demons."

Well, color him impressed. Seemed he'd be getting the full royal treatment.

The door opened and the largest man he'd ever seen walked in—and that was really saying something considering how huge Demetri was. Alex had seen Varrick before, when they fought Eldrick together in Siberia and when he and Stephan sat down to discuss matters, but here the king seemed immense.

Perhaps being in his own element made Varrick stand taller, but Alex couldn't help but be a little intimidated by his presence. His blond hair was worn slightly longer than typical for a warrior. The red eyes on the thick face and the blond five o'clock shadow that met his stare seemed more beastial than man. He exhibited a lionesque appearance about him.

"Good evening, Alexander," the king greeted as he handed the woman into one of the chairs on the dais.

"Please, call me Alex." The Alpha compared the king and queen. Their only similarity was their sandy hair. Aside from that, they were complete physical opposites.

She was quite small, a petite slip of a girl with golden eyes which matched her long hair. Elizabeth was a pretty thing, not at all animal-like. And Alex wondered what she saw in Varrick.

"Very well, Alex, it is then." Varrick clasped the queen's hand in his after he too sat.

Alex moved closer to the dais while Cyrus remained back and to the side. The Alpha's eyes darted between him and Varrick briefly before he spoke. "And what should I call you?"

The king seemed to ponder the question for a moment. "You may call me Varrick. Allow me to introduce my mate, Elizabeth."

Alex reached his right hand forward and took a step toward the woman, intending to shake her hand. A low growl from Varrick stopped him in his tracks. He lowered his hand immediately. *No touching the queen. Got it.*

"It is nice to meet you, Alex," Elizabeth stated with a smile. "You'll have to forgive Varrick. He can be a little possessive."

"A little?" Cyrus mumbled so low Alex was sure only his preternatural hearing picked it up.

Varrick cleared his throat. "As Stephan and I agreed, I have arranged lodging for you here in my compound."

"I appreciate that. I'll try not to be too much of a bother."

Elizabeth crossed her legs. "I'm sure you won't be any bother at all. To be sure you have everything you need, we've found someone to help you."

That didn't sound good. The last thing Alex needed was a big burly babysitter. Having someone watching over his shoulder might hinder his recon.

"That won't be necessary. I won't need much help," he assured the couple.

"I insist." Varrick's eyes narrowed as if daring Alex to descent again. "After all, we can't have you roaming the place, getting lost, now can we. We found someone who will be very useful…to you. Someone who can run errands, help you install the communication equipment. Help you navigate around this place until you get your bearings."

Alex could only imagine who they'd pick for the job. *Probably Cyrus, since he remained in this room, or more likely Caden, because they obviously don't trust me. Smart demons*.

The door opening behind him heralded a presence. Before he turned to look, a familiar scent filled his nose. Sunshine and roses. Instantly, his mind conjured the image of a lithe body being held up against a tree by his hand. He resisted the urge to cover his tingling groin as he remembered the pain from a knee hitting it. Then the mental scene flashed to Tatiana holding a naked form against a warehouse in Canada. His groin tingled again, this time for a very different reason.

With snow-white hair down to her waist, the demon had looked beautiful. Her pale body glistened in the moonlight. They might have been pumping her for information at the time, but Alex was still a male, and he'd found the demon attractive, even if she'd just kneed him in the family jewels to escape him before Tatiana got a hold of her.

He turned slowly, watching Shira enter the room, her hair swishing behind her as she sauntered. Her medium frame held womanly curves but was not overweight. Her piercing eyes, red with flecks of gold, locked with his.

"Hello," she said casually as if they'd never met.

Did she not remember him? He certainly remembered her, *all* of her. The muscle of his jaw flexed.

"Hello, Shira," he replied. Alex observed her face, looking for any hint of surprise that he remembered her name. She showed none. Perhaps she *did* remember they were already acquainted.

"Do you two know each other?" Varrick asked.

"In a manner of speaking," Alex replied, his gaze returning to the king.

Shira stepped beside him. "We met in Canada."

A knowing expression passed quickly over Varrick's face. The king was obviously aware of what happened at the warehouse in Canada when the demons had been torturing Demetri. That SOB probably authorized it. Which reminded Alex these demons should not be trusted.

"Good then. No introductions are necessary." Varrick eased forward in his chair. "Shira, show Alex around. Make him…feel at home."

The female demon curtsied; her eyes cast down to the ground. "Of course, my lord. I will see to it the vampire is taken care of."

Alex didn't like the sound of that.

## Chapter 3

Alex strolled along, his duffle bag slung over one shoulder and the cooler of blood in his other hand. The Alpha shortened his strides to match his companion while avoiding bumping into her in the narrow hall.

Sconces hung on the granite walls. The torches within flickered and flared, blown by a breeze.

*I wonder how they ventilate this place.* He glanced behind him and saw only more rocky hallway.

They passed one nondescript door after the next until they came upon one that stood opened.

"What's that?" he asked, slowing his strides to peek inside.

Little ones scampered about the colorfully decorated space, playing with toys while a woman placed food on a short table. A quick count and Alex realized fifteen children were present.

*Sixteen,* he amended silently as a tiny, white-haired boy emerged from what Alex assumed was a bathroom, struggling to snap his pants.

"That's none of your business." Shira closed the door.

As they resumed their trek down the walkway, Alex cleared his throat. "What a big bunch of rug rats."

Did the demons conceive more easily than vampires?

"You leave them alone," Shira snapped.

Alex stopped, going stone still. He waited until Shira halted and faced him, determined to look her in the eye. "You believe I'd harm a child?"

He didn't bother keeping the disbelief or anger from his voice.

The female demon crossed her arms over her chest. "Quite frankly, I don't know what you're capable of, vampire. If I remember correctly, the last time we met, you pinned me to a tree by my throat."

Guilt socked him hard in the breadbasket. *Shit!*

Alex put the cooler down and shifted uncomfortably from foot to foot, realizing he needed to set things right. He wasn't the kind of male to hurt a woman—an enemy though was another thing. How could he explain the difference to her?

Alex ran a hand through his short hair then rubbed the back of his neck. "Yeah, about that—"

Shira held up a hand. "Don't bother explaining. I know you and…that woman you were with were looking for your friend. But your tactics sucked, especially for me. And just when I thought I was getting past it, you show up here."

"I'm sorry." It wouldn't be enough, but it was a start.

"I don't want any apologies. Do what you're here to do and go, so I don't have to have you around as a constant reminder of what happened."

With that, Shira turned and resumed her lithe strides down the hall, leaving Alex no choice but to grab the cooler and follow.

****

The last embers of the fire died, taking with them the only light. The damp, musty odor of the cave pushed in on Jara, and her stomach threaten to expel the meager meal she and Eldrick had shared.

"How much longer are we going to have to stay here?" She wrapped her arms around her waist in a bracing hug.

"Why? Do you not like my company, *Schadenfreude*?" The voice oozed over her in the darkness, covering her skin like malevolent tar.

He knew damned well she didn't like his company. How could she? He was a bloodsucker, a sick bastard who treated her without thoughtfulness since fate joined them in that Siberian grotto. But as long as he was talking, he wasn't hurting her—usually.

"What did you call me?"

"*Schadenfreude*. It means a person who derives pleasure from the misfortunes or pain of others. It is a befitting name for one such as you, is it not?"

A shiver raced from the rock floor up her spine. His evil laugh filled the small space. She'd tried to escape, but somehow, he always preempted her attempts.

"We are so close to the city? Why must we stay in the cave when we could easily get a room at a nice hotel? Wouldn't you prefer a bed to sleep in?"

"Not really. This cave served as my home for years. The forest provides me what little sustenance I require. The stream provides fresh water."

"But I need more to eat than you do. The small animals we've shared each night are not enough. Besides, wouldn't you love some Chinese food? Maybe Kung Pao Chicken."

Jara's stomach rumbled its agreement.

"What is this Kung Pao Chicken?"

"That's right. You've been in stasis for—" Jara let the rest of the sentence drop.

She didn't wish to remind him of the centuries he'd spent lying unconscious in Siberia. He'd made it quite clear he blamed her and her kind for his misfortune, and he had the right to do so, for it had been a group of powerful demons who bespelled the bloodsucker and left him there to rot until she'd had the brilliant idea of finding him to kill him.

"Come here." Hate filled the tone of his voice, and she shrank against the hard rock wall. "I'm ready for dessert."

When she didn't move, Eldrick's presence filled her mind, taking all thought. Her body uncurled and moved forward at his will. She fought, like she always did, to no avail.

Since the cave was too small to stand in, Jara crawled on her hands and knees. The hard surface bit into her legs, and she whimpered, earning another laugh from her captor. Her throat constricted with sorrow, and tears flowed from her eyes. Her kneecaps landed in their trail when she moved, adding to her misery. It took mere seconds to make the journey, but dread of what would come made time slow.

Once she reached Eldrick, he forced her to bow before him. When her arm jutted out in offering, his icy fingers clamped around her wrist, hard enough to flex the bones. Pain shot up her arm, but it would only get worse. His hot, foul breath fanned over her skin. She fought his control, tried to push him from her mind, but it was no use.

His fangs sank deep into the delicate crook of her arm, and the excruciating pain forced a sorrowful cry between her pressed lips. He drew deeply, sucking her flesh and blood into his mouth with stinging force. She grew lightheaded, the cave spun. She swayed.

Eldrick's grip tightened, holding her while he drank his fill. Slurping sounds filled her ears until at last, he licked the wound closed and released her arm. She fell against the hard ground in a heap. Having no strength to catch herself, her head smacked the rock, sending a fresh round of pain screaming through her brain.

It was a small price to pay to finally be away from his touch.

Jara's ears rang. Blinded by the darkness in the cave, she realized he'd moved only when she felt him lift her head.

He shoved his wrist against her mouth. "Drink."

"No," she muttered and pushed weakly against his arm.

His presence again filled her mind, forced her mouth open. The coppery tang of blood flowed over her tongue. Jara gagged, tried to force her mouth away, but he refused to allow it. She swallowed the vile stuff.

It burned her throat, and her stomach knotted as it tried to refuse the blood entry. White-hot heat scorched every cell. When her throat threatened to close, she coughed.

"Drink," he repeated and pressed his wrist more firmly against her teeth.

Jara took five more swallows. Something clicked in her brain. A subtle snap like a rubber band and then an oily film coated her mind.

*Stop.*

Suddenly, she regained control of her body. Eldrick

released her. Jara scampered back, uncaring where she went. She just needed to put distance between them. After wiping her mouth with the back of her hand, she spit.

*You should not waste my gift.*

Terror widened her eyes, and she covered her mouth. His voice didn't echo off the cave walls. Instead, it sounded in her head.

"What did you do?" Fear made her shiver.

*Created a mindlink. Now I no longer need to communicate like a mortal. I can speak to you as a vampire should.*

"A mind what?"

*Mindlink. And you don't need to talk. You can use this channel to communicate with me as I do you.*

Her mind struggled to grasp the significance of what transpired. She didn't want to be linked in any way with this psychopath.

*That's not nice. Guard your thoughts.*

He heard that?

*Yes, I did.*

If he could hear her every thought, she was in serious trouble.

*Yes, you are.*

The blackness in the cave eased until she clearly saw the vampire across the way. His eyes narrowed; the corner of his lips rose revealing one fang in a sneer of a smile. The male appeared like evil incarnate. Oh, Goddess help her.

*Your Goddess cannot save you now. You are mine to command. I know all your thoughts, have complete control over you.*

Terror devoured her body, and Jara vomited.

## Chapter 4

Alex sent his awareness out while he walked silently beside Shira. He found numerous blank spots. Demetri had warned him thick veins of titanium ran through the mountain. The mineral and the amount of demons living within left little for his senses to pick up.

He'd have to do some old-fashion recon. Eyes-on would be the way to get intel in here. Luckily, Varrick assigned a female to escort him. Perhaps he might charm her into a tour.

After going through more twists and turns than he'd find in a corn maze, Shira finally stopped before a wooden door.

"This is your room." The demon opened the door.

Alex crossed the threshold and took in the meager lodgings. A small dresser rested against one of the rock walls while a wooden chair sat between the two lit torches in sconces. A bunk bed, with neatly folded sheets stacked at the foot of the mattress, completed the jail cell motif.

"Looks like the maid forgot to make the bed," Alex quipped with a grin.

"Perhaps the bloodsucker would prefer a coffin?" Shira murmured under her breath.

No doubt she didn't realize Alex's acute hearing picked up every word. So much for charming her into a tour. Guess he'd have to find his own way around this place, and to do that he needed to get rid of her.

"Thanks for showing me to my room. I think I'll turn in." Alex put his duffle bag on the dresser, then placed his cooler on the floor.

Shira eyed the cooler. "What's in there?"

"Sustenance." Alex flashed his most disarming smile.

"As in blood?" Her eyes widened, and revulsion took her face.

He nodded.

"That's disgusting."

"You never know, until you try it."

"Don't be crass. Drinking blood is only one of the things about being a vampire that is gross."

Alex raised a questioning eyebrow. "*One* of the things? Care to enlighten me about what the others might be?"

He crossed his arms over his chest.

"Well, for starters you all stink."

Alex lifted one arm and took a loud sniff of his pit. "I beg your pardon. I do not smell."

"All vampires have an odor. Demons can smell them a mile away. Some more than others, but they all stink."

*Good to know*, thought Alex. "I'll try to keep my stench to a minimum. Is that the only thing you don't like?"

Shira blew out a heavy sigh, letting her lids close over her beautiful eyes for a few seconds as if she gathered her thoughts. When she pinned Alex with her fiery stare, it took all his self-control not to flinch from the daggers shot at him.

"Look, let's not pretend Canada didn't happen. I

don't care for you. You are a bully, a jerk, and no doubt you believe you can use your pretty-boy looks to charm your way out of any situation."

"Pretty-boy? You think I'm *pretty*?" How offensive. Powerful, muscular, even handsome would have sounded better. But pretty?

Alex shook his head.

"Figures that would be the word you keyed in on. I also mentioned bully and jerk, in case you missed those."

He hadn't missed them. In fact, they stung like titanium bullets when she said them. He understood why she saw him that way, but those particular terms were not what he wanted her to think.

Alex needed to get her on his side. If Shira was his keeper, he needed to disarm her. He'd have to do serious damage control to get her to see the real him. And given her obvious dislike of vampires, he had his work cut out for him.

"I have decent hearing. I didn't miss those terms. But I believe you have me all wrong." Alex covered his heart with his hand. "I'm a lover, not a fighter."

A brash scoffing noise pushed from Shira's throat.

"Well, okay, I'm a fighter too, but I'm really not a horrible guy. We got off on the wrong foot. Get to know me better. You might like me."

He moved until only a few inches separated them. Shira took a step back, and Alex followed, his predatory instincts honing in. When her back hit the wall, there were mere inches separating them. Heat radiated from her small, supple body. Her breathing increased. Her pulse quickened beneath her pale flesh.

Alex leaned in and whispered, "I'd certainly like to

get to know you a little better."

Her hands pushed against his chest, burning like a brand. She dodged around him and made a beeline for the door.

Yanking it open, she paused then turned to face him. "Stay in this room. I'll come by tomorrow to show you around."

"I sleep late and might be in bed when you come back. You should know I sleep in the nude."

Shira's cheeks reddened as she mumbled, "Of course you do," and left. The door slammed behind her.

Alex chuckled. Mission accomplished. The teasing worked. She was gone. It was time to do a little exploring.

****

Three purposeful strides took Shira to her room. Varrick had put the vampire next to her. Just her luck. Not only did she have to babysit the guy, but even at night, she couldn't get away from him. He was her responsibility 24/7 which sucked.

She kicked off her shoes and let the sparks fly from her fingers to light the logs in the fireplace, then plopped down on the couch in front of the fire. The crackling flames comforted her. While the flames danced, her mind wandered to thoughts of the vampire.

She still felt his warm breath against her ear. A shiver raced through her. He wasn't exactly ugly with those baby-blue eyes and blond hair that begged to have fingers run through it. He was well built, muscular with broad shoulders that tapered to a narrow waist. The man exuded confidence. Too much so.

She'd have to be careful. It would be easy to succumb to his affable charm. She almost did so when he pinned her up against the wall. Luckily, his vampiric odor surrounded her bringing her out of the stupor, and she'd come to her senses before she gave into the temptation his lips presented.

Shira pressed her hand to her mouth and shook her head in an attempt to dislodge the lust from her brain.

"I need to get it together."

"Why?"

The sound of Talia's voice pulled Shira from her reverie. She glanced over her shoulder and found her twin sister standing with an arm full of toys.

"I didn't hear you come in," Shira stated, hoping to change the subject. Her eyes landed on the open door before pinning her sister with a pointed stare. "You should have knocked or something."

"Since when have I needed to knock?" She crossed the room, putting the playthings in the open toybox under the table resting against the back of the couch. Coming around the sofa, she continued, "What's got you in such a snit?"

"Nothing." Shira wasn't in the mood to talk about it.

"Yeah, right. Spill."

Apparently, Talia wasn't going to let it drop. Perhaps she needed a bigger distraction.

"Where's Tyler?"

"Still in daycare. When I stopped by to pick him up, he asked for more time to play. I couldn't deny him when he gave me those sweet puppy-dog eyes."

Shira knew that look well. Her nephew had used it since he was around a week old, and over the past four years, he'd perfected it. Too bad the boy's father wasn't still here to see it. If only he'd stayed away from humans and hadn't caught the flu, he'd still be here to see his little boy grow up.

"What's with the toys?"

"I thought you might want some new ones since Tyler is over here so often."

Shira laughed. "You mean you were running out of space at your place, so you thought you'd make room by bringing these toys over here and cluttering up my room."

Talia rolled her eyes. "Whatever." Her warm smile reached her red eyes. "You know me so well."

"That I do."

"And I know you too, sis. So, spill. I know you were upset when I got here. What's going on?"

Shira settled back on the couch. "It's the bloodsucker."

"The vampire Varrick assigned you to watch?"

"Yeah. He's a pain in the butt."

"He didn't try to hurt you again, did he? I'll kill him." Talia's hands balled into fists.

Shira laid a hand on her sister's arm. "He behaved himself."

"Then what is it that has you so worked up?"

And wasn't that the million-dollar question? Shira couldn't exactly put her finger on it. Alex had been polite enough, even a little flirtatious. But he hadn't crossed a line, not really. Yet he got her dander up in a way few did.

"I don't exactly know. He's just—" Knocking on her door halted the remainder of her sentence.

"Who is it?" she called out.

"Alex. I have a question for you."

Talia's eyes went round. "He sounds yummy."

"Hide. I don't want him to see you."

"Why not?"

Shira stood, pulling Talia with her. She gave her a shove toward the bathroom. "Go in there. Don't come out until I tell you."

"But—" Shira pushed her inside the bath and closed the door. Quickly crossing the room, she pulled open the door and barely contained a gasp.

Alex stood bare-chested, a towel hung over one shoulder. His jeans rode low on his hips. She forced her eyes away from them, trailing over his corrugated abs and chiseled pecs. The muscles striated across his middle and cut so deep they created shadows. His thick biceps flexed when he removed the towel from his shoulder and draped it around his neck. Each hand grabbed an end of the cloth, and for a brief moment, she wished those hands were grabbing her instead.

Her eyes slowly traveled up to his full lips before skirting to the dimple in his left cheek and finally locking with his aquamarine eyes, those very, very blue eyes. His was a handsome face in an all-American kind of way. She swallowed hard.

"Can I help you?" she squeaked out.

A knowing grin raised the corners of his mouth and the arrogance lit her anger.

"I wondered if you might show me where the showers are. It's been a long night, and I want to get cleaned up before bed. You know, so I don't stink." Alex winked, and Shira almost smiled.

An image of him bathing in the falls, soapy bubbles sliding down his physique, played in her mind's eye. Goddess help her. Why did she keep having this reaction around him? For some reason, he set her blood on fire. And she didn't need *or* want that.

She'd have to accompany him to the bath. Varrick instructed her not to leave him alone. Somehow, she'd hadn't thought about him needing to get cleaned up. Shira made a mental note to come up with a way to address the situation in the future that didn't involve her.

"I can show you. Hold on while I grab my shoes."

"Can you grab me some soap too?"

Shira closed Alex out in the hallway and ran to her bathroom. The door opened wide when she approached.

"Great Goddess bless us, he's gorgeous!" her sister exclaimed, handing Shira a bar of perfumed soap.

"Shhhh. He'll hear you." Shira snatched the soap. "How did you see him, anyway?"

"I peeked."

"Did he see you?"

"No." Talia licked her lips. "I want to meet him."

"Later, sis. Another day."

"You embarrassed of me, Shira?"

"No." Really, she didn't know why, but she didn't wish to share her family with the vampire yet.

"You worried about a little competition? Worried I'll steal him from you?"

Shira moved to the bed, placed the bar of soap on the comforter and grabbed her shoes. "My Goddess, no. I can't stand the jerk."

Talia smiled. "Right. That's why your cheeks are flushed, and you sounded like a young girl when you were talking to him."

"I did not," Shira denied as she donned her shoes.

"Hold on I'll show you where the shower is," her sister teased in a high-pitched voice. "And if you don't mind, I'll just stand there and watch while you take off all your clothes and wash."

Shira gave her sister a playful push then grabbed the soap. "Shut up. He'll hear you."

"He can't hear me through the closed door."

"Doesn't matter. Now close the bathroom door so I can leave."

Talia shot her a girl-you-are-in-*so*-much-trouble look and complied.

Shira opened the door to discover the vampire faced away. Her gaze roamed his back in a slow perusal, taking in the defined lines of his muscles.

"Ready?"

Alex turned around and nodded. "Sure."

Closing the door behind her, Shira swore she heard her sister whisper have fun.

She led him through the hall, making the first right down the corridor which led to the communal bath.

"This place is really impressive," Alex shared. "Did I see your room has a fireplace?"

"So?" Shira quickened her strides to keep up with his long legs.

"So, how can you have a fire inside a mountain? Where does the smoke go?"

"I'm not sure."

"But it must go somewhere, or it would fill the room. Do most of the rooms here have fireplaces?"

"Yeah. Most do."

"So, then there must be some kind of ventilation system. But if so, what happens to the smoke? I mean it would have to go somewhere. I didn't see any smoke coming out of the mountain when I approached."

"I don't know."

Alex ran a hand through his hair. Shira tracked the movement, marveling at how it fell back into place, feathered on his forehead. She wondered if it would be as soft as it appeared.

Augh! Shira immediately clamped down on her stray thoughts. This vampire was her enemy. A sexy enemy but an enemy none the less.

"But the smoke—"

"Look, I don't know anything about the ventilation system in this place. We have fire, we breathe, and no smoke can be seen. End of story. Now leave it alone," she barked, irritation from the betrayal of her own thoughts hardening her voice. It was much safer to remain angry with the guy. Anger took away any lust.

"Do you know who might know? I'd like to speak to someone about it."

"Why, so you can figure out a way to make it stop working and suffocate us?"

The vampire stopped on a dime and gave her an incredulous look. "Where did that come from?"

*Good question.* "Forget it. Come on. The bath is only a little further."

Alex didn't move. "I didn't come here to hurt anyone."

Shira's fisted hands found her hips. "Why did you come here?"

"To help."

"A vampire help demons? I doubt that very much."

"Have I given you any reason not to trust me?"

"Not yet." *But you will*, she reminded herself. Vampires can't be trusted. An image of him choking her flashed in her mind. "Actually, I remember your hand squeezing around my neck. You were pretty intimidating that night."

Alex blanched. "I tried to explain earlier. That night I was in fight mode. I didn't mean you any harm."

"Sure seemed as if you and that woman you were with intended to harm me. In fact, I remember you threatening me."

"Actually, what I said was I recommend you stop fighting Tatiana and answer her questions."

Shira shrugged. "So, the threat was implied. It was still a threat."

Alex appeared to ponder that. His face softened.

"You're right," he conceded. "I apologize. My friend was in trouble and getting answers from you was the only way we were going to find him."

"Shhhh." Shira glanced around to be sure no one heard him. No one realized she was the reason Alex and the female vampire found their warehouse in Canada. And she certainly didn't want that getting back to Varrick. He'd have her head—or worse. "Forget it. It's over and done with. I don't want to talk about it."

"Does that mean you forgive me?"

"Yeah, sure, if it means we don't have to talk about it anymore." Shira moved forward, and Alex followed on her heels.

"Why don't I believe you?" he asked.

"Believe whatever you want," she tossed over her shoulder. "We're here."

She'd never been so glad to see a door in her life. The demonic symbol painted on the wood signified it was the bath for males.

"Through this door, Alex, you'll find the bath."

He cocked a light eyebrow. "You aren't coming?"

A blush heated her face.

"Absolutely not." She forced the bar of soap into his hand. "It's for males only."

"Too bad," he murmured. An impish grin lifted one corner of his mouth, flashing his dimple. "I kinda hoped you were going to stand there and watch."

Her sister's earlier words sprang to mind as did the image they invoked. That southern drawl had a way of pulling her in, made her long to be out under the stars with only him for company.

Goddess help her, he'd done it again.

"I don't think so, cowboy."

"I'm not a cowboy, darlin'. But anytime you want a wild ride, I'd be happy to oblige." He gave her a wink and sauntered into the bath, closing the door behind him.

Holy Hell that man could be infuriating.

Indecision made her pace. Should she wait for him? Varrick would probably want her to. But if she did, she'd have to spend more time with him tonight, and she'd had enough.

One minute he was exasperating and the next charming. And the way he slung sexual innuendoes…Well, she had to admit those were sort of fun, but still. She didn't need the temptation he represented. She'd been assigned to keep an eye on him, but she hadn't been told to spend every waking minute in his presence.

Decision made, she headed back to her room to what was sure to be a good ribbing from her sister.

# Chapter 5

Alex tossed the sheets off his body and sat up in bed. He ran his fingers roughly through his hair. The flowery soap aroma lingered in the room as it had the previous five nights. That girly soap had a way of sticking with him, but he didn't mind. It seemed to mask the vampire scent, at least according to Shira, which could only help when doing recon. And he could use all the help he could get.

He'd been here almost a week and had little intel to show for it. The woman never left him alone. Every night she'd follow him into what was now being called the communications room and watch as he tried to bring this compound into the twenty-first century.

Alex rolled from the bed, donned his jeans and sweater in a hurry, and hoped he'd awakened early enough that Shira might not expect him. The alpha cracked the door and peered out.

*Success!*

He closed the door behind him and traipsed down the hall. Seemed like a good night to do some exploring. A smile raised the corners of his mouth.

He moved through the halls with an easy stride, hoping he appeared as if he belonged there.

The sideways glances he got from the demons he passed told him he didn't.

*Whatever.* As long as they left him alone, they

could think anything they wanted. While he continued down the dimly lit hall, he sent his senses out, more from habit than necessity, and found a whole lot of nothing, as usual.

Familiar sounds of metal meeting metal drew him like a kid to an ice cream truck. Excitement bubbled in his blood when the smell of grease and transmission fluid filled his sinuses. He stopped before a set of swinging doors, sure of what lay beyond.

Alex pushed tentatively through the entry into an impressive garage. Before him stood a row of motorcycles and behind them a line a cars and trucks. Lining the rock walls around the room, stood large toolboxes.

“Can I help you?” a burly demon with pitch-black hair asked from across the cavernous room. He straightened then wiped his hands on a rag. The male appeared as tired as a rusted-out chassis.

“Just checking things out,” Alex called back. “Nice garage you got here.”

The demon made his way over to Alex. “Why are you here?”

Not exactly a friendly type. But Alex would fix that. Nothing brought car guys together like talking shop.

“I wanted to see your set up. I have a couple of auto repair places.” The demon’s eyebrows rose in interest, so Alex continued. “One of them is a tranny place. Perhaps you’ve heard of it, Bleed ‘em Dry Transmission.”

“You own a Bleed ‘em Dry? That’s the largest retail chain of transmission shops in the country. So, where’s your shop?”

The demon sounded impressed, and Alex appreciated that. "All across the country. I started the franchise."

"So, you're like a CEO or something?"

"Something like that." The demon's face soured. "But I still get my hands dirty," Alex added quickly, knowing most mechanics appreciated someone who worked with their hands.

"Huh." The demon seemed unimpressed.

"I'm Alex, by the way." His hand shot out, and the demon grasped it in a firm grip before shaking it.

"Name's Dominious, but everyone calls me Dom."

"So, Dom, what were you working on before I got here?"

"That old pickup over there." He gestured toward a black truck with his thumb. "Damned thing keeps slipping gears."

A genuine smile reached Alex's eyes. "Sounds like the transmission. Need any help dropping it?"

Dom gave him the once over. "You aren't exactly dressed for pulling a tranny."

Alex removed his sweater. "I am now."

The demon nodded. "Well, all right then. I can always use a little help."

Anticipation mixed with excitement. Alex couldn't wait to get under the vehicle. Nothing cleared the mind like being under two tons of metal, your fingers slick with fluids. You had to keep your wits about you, or you might get hurt. This was exactly what he needed to get his mind off his sexy little keeper, Shira.

Two hours later, having installed the new transmission, Alex stood on the bumper of the truck, leaning over into the engine compartment, a wrench in one hand and spark plugs in the other with perspiration dripping off his body. It felt good to break a sweat, do a little hard labor.

"What in Hades are you doing *here*?" A familiar voice yelled. "Do you have any idea how many people are looking for you?"

Alex laid the wrench and plugs on the car's battery, unfolded from the vehicle and grabbed a towel. He wiped his hands and arms as he turned to face Shira. The fiery demon stood with her hands fisted on her hips and an expression on her face that would have quelled a less confident male.

"Miss me darlin'?" The alpha gave her what he hoped was a disarming smile.

Her eyes traveled his body, and her demeanor softened. Good. Perhaps he affected this little demon as much as she affected him.

"I-I…"

Alex's mouth twitched when her eyes fell back to his damp chest and remained there.

"Should I put a shirt on?" he asked, fighting to keep a straight face.

Shira's pretty face flushed a deep red, and she inhaled a slow breath before she spoke. "No! Yes! Er…I mean, do whatever you want. I don't care."

*Fates, it's fun to tease this woman*, thought Alex.

He draped the towel on the truck and turned back to the engine. "Okay then. I won't."

He pulled the engine. His muscle strained from the weight when he carried it over to a bench. Alex felt her eyes roam his body as he moved. A grin took his face. Pulling tools from the large yellow toolbox next to the workbench, he removed the bolts.

"You want to use the compressor to do that?" asked Dom.

"Naw." His preternatural strength would get the job done, plus it would seem more impressive to the little demon watching him with her bottom lip pulled between her teeth.

"So, what brings you here, Shira?" *As if I didn't know.*

"I was told to keep…I-I just wondered where you were."

*Told to keep an eye on me is more likely.* Why else would she have stuck to him like glue every second he'd been here? He really shouldn't complain. As guards went, she was a good-looking one, even if she needed an attitude adjustment now and then.

"Well, you found me."

"Yeah, after searching around for hours. Why aren't you in the communications room working on the computers?"

He shrugged. "I can't do anything more until we figure out a way to cool the room, so the server won't overheat."

"Then shouldn't you be thinking about that instead of messing about down here in the garage?" Shira accused hotly.

"I'll have you know I do my best thinking under a car." Perspiration trickled down his chest. Hunger flashed in Shira's eyes as they followed the trail. Damn, it was fun getting her all riled up.

"And have you come up with a solution?" Shira moved a little closer as if she was afraid to get too near.

"I might have. Give me a little while longer to reason it through." He grabbed two bottles of water from the top of the toolbox. "Want a drink?"

Shira took the one he offered. He tipped the other to his mouth and drained it in long swallows, allowing her a lengthy stare at him standing there half naked, head tipped back. Alex heard a soft moan push through her lips and struggled not to smile around the bottle. She enjoyed playing the pissed off demon, but he preferred the flirty one and wasn't above using what the Fates gave him to bring that out.

****

Goddess help her, he had a body that made her drool. Alex drained the plastic bottle. His Adam's apple bobbed in his thick, corded neck. It reminded her of how the muscles rippled under his skin when he hauled the engine out of the truck and brought it to the table. Her body warmed at the memory.

*Damn it!*

She didn't want this attraction, tried to make it perfectly clear she didn't care for him, but when he turned on that flirty charm and sexy grin, she couldn't help but flirt back. And Talia didn't help. Her sister continually suggested she take advantage of being assigned to watch the handsome man and take the vampire to her bed.

*As if that would ever happen.* Ogling a vampire was one thing, but sleeping with him?

Not going to happen.

"Are you going to drink that water, or just fondle it all day?" Alex asked, gracing her with a toothy grin.

Confusion squinted her fiery eyes, and she glanced down to discover she'd been unconsciously running her hand up and down the water bottle. Her cheeks heated in a blush.

A chuckle drew her eyes to Dom.

"I'm going to go grab a bite to eat. Want to join me?" he asked. Not waiting for a reply, he headed for the doors.

Alex gave her a pointed look, his eyes dropping to her neck. "I *am* feeling rather hungry."

Her hand flew to her throat. "Well then, I guess we'd better go to the cafeteria, and get you something to eat."

"I didn't say I was hungry for food, now did I?" Alex bantered, with a wag of his blond brows.

Shira rolled her eyes. "Well, that's all I'm offering."

Alex affected a hurt expression and placed a hand over his heart. "I'm crushed. A man cannot survive on food alone. I thought you were supposed to see to my every need while I'm here."

If Talia had her way, that's exactly what Shira would do, but luckily, she was in control and didn't plan on satisfying any of the vampire's needs. "Your needs are your problem."

His mouth twitched into a half smile. "Then I guess I will have to take care of them myself."

Her mind betrayed her with an image of Alex lying naked on a bed, his hand working his most manly part. Shira's core heated, belly tightened. Her tongue darted out to lick suddenly dry lips.

A bestial growl emanated from the vampire, and her gaze flew to his. Hunger burned in his eyes. He stalked toward her, making her back up until her bottom touched the cool metal of a toolbox.

Her breath quickened, heart raced. He stopped mere inches from her and placed his hands on either side, gripping the box to wall her in.

"There's something you should know." His gravelly voice, low and heavy, carried a sensual tone.

Though afraid to ask, curiosity got the better of her. "What's that?"

"I can sense your attraction to me. Have for days."

"I'm not—" Her false protest died when his lips met hers.

Fireworks exploded; the blood rushed to her ears drowning out everything but the sound of her heart beating. Shira's eyes closed of their own volition when her fingers laced behind his neck.

His tongue pushed between her lips. His arm curled around her back and pulled her against his heat. Shira's mouth opened wide in welcome, wanting his exploration. Alex's lips pressed against hers with a passion which would not be denied, and Goddess help her, she didn't want to deny him.

She wanted to give in to the passion. Give into him. The temptation he presented threatened to consume her. A woman could get lost in his kiss, his touch.

A small moan sounded in his throat. The arm behind her back tightened as his fingers bunched in her hair.

He took control, angling her head to deepen their kiss when he pushed her against the toolbox. Shira's heart beat so hard, surely, he felt it. Any minute it would push through her ribs, but she didn't care. All she cared about in that moment was him.

Alex pulled his lips from hers and feathered tiny kisses along her jaw, down her throat. He suckled against the flesh where her neck met her shoulder. Shira tilted her head to give him better access. Her hand wandered into his hair; fingers wove through the silky strands. His hair felt as soft as she'd imagined.

His tongue danced over her skin. Goosebumps pimpled her flesh. Teeth scraped her skin, and she anticipated the bite that would mark her as his.

The realization jarred her out of the passionate stupor. What the Hell was she doing? He wasn't a demon ready to mark a mate, he was a vampire seeking a lunch. Panic flooded her body with adrenaline, and she shoved at his chest with all her might.

Alex staggered back, his fangs on display when he hissed.

"Don't you hiss at me, you pervert." Shira crossed her arms over her chest.

"Pervert? Sweetheart, I didn't hear you complaining."

"You were going to *bite* me," she accused fiercely.

"I was not." Alex scrubbed a hand through his thick hair. "Okay, maybe I was going to take a tiny taste."

"I'm not on the menu, buddy."

"I'm sorry. I don't know what got into me. I haven't consumed any blood today, and the energy I expended working on the truck must have depleted me."

She held a hand out when he approached. "Don't come any closer."

The hurt on his face softened her resolve. "I'd never hurt you, Shira."

"You almost did," she reminded him, dropping her arms to her sides.

"It wouldn't have hurt. In fact, it can be quite

pleasurable."

"I'd rather not find out if it is all the same to you."

She didn't miss his hands fisting against his thighs as if he struggled to keep from touching her. Or perhaps he was angry, she wasn't sure which. If she had to be with Alex, the more people around the better.

"I believe we should go find Dom in the cafeteria." Shira shifted.

Alex hesitated, then blew out a heavy sigh and with a defeated expression said, "Fine. Let's go."

## Chapter 6

Alex followed Shira down the hall, unable to keep his eyes from the sway of her hips. His hunger stirred at the sight, and he scraped a hand down his face.

What was it about that demon? The moment their lips touched he'd wanted a taste of her blood something fierce. But surely, it was simply because he'd neglected to consume blood prior to going down to the shop.

His lips still tingled from their kiss. He ran his tongue over them, tasting their passion. He'd never wanted anything as much as he'd wanted her. When they'd touched something took over his body, pushing all rational thoughts from his mind. He became more animal than man, a beast wanting to take the woman before him, rip the clothes from her and have his way with her as he sank his fangs deep with her neck and drank. A tremor shimmied through him.

After they rounded the corner, Shira preceded the Alpha into the large dining facility. As usual, his eyes roamed the room, taking in every nuance. It appeared similar to a military style mess hall. Several wooden tables with bench seating accommodated the guests. In the back, stood a serving counter with a medieval kitchen behind it.

A small marble table and four padded chairs sat at the head of the room. Varrick and Elizabeth eating there confirmed his suspicions. The special seating was reserved for the king and queen.

As Shira and Alex made their way through the cafeteria line, he watched the business behind the counter. The cooks and servers worked in perfect synchronicity. They hustled throughout the kitchen. A man washed vegetables at a sink carved in the stone wall and then handed them one by one to a woman chopping at the counter. Three males manned the wood-burning stoves, stoking the fires and turning the meat as it cooked. In a choreographed dance, the workers moved this way and that, somehow avoiding each other while they stirred about the space.

Alex pushed his tray down the line and plucked an apple from a bowl. Shira, on the other hand, loaded her plate full of potatoes, roast beef, and a pile of steamed veggies. The woman sure could eat, and he wondered where it all went in her thin body. Alex chuckled.

Shira shot him a scathing glance over her shoulder. "What's so funny, cowboy?"

"I told you, I'm not a cowboy." Alex took a bite of apple.

Shira huffed, grabbed her tray and headed toward Dom. As she settled beside him, Alex traveled in the opposite direction. After giving his unnecessary tray to a demon getting in line, he approached the king, apple in hand.

"Hey, Varrick."

The male's eyes slowly rose as he chewed and swallowed his food. "Greetings, Alex."

"Hello, Alex," Elizabeth chimed in with a wave.

The Alpha smiled. "Hi, Elizabeth. Mind if I pull up a chair?"

Without waiting for a reply, Alex chose the seat

across from Elizabeth and beside Varrick.

"Make yourself at home." Varrick eyed him cautiously as he eased back in his chair and crossed his thick arms over his massive chest. "Is there something I can do for you?"

His tone told Alex the offer wasn't coming from a place of hospitality, and the Alpha decided he'd better say his piece and go, right quick. "I've been thinking, and I don't believe we're going to be able to house the servers in this compound."

"Why not?" asked Varrick.

"It's not cool enough. We need to put them someplace with an AC you can turn way down. And for AC we'll need electricity."

"We don't have electricity," Elizabeth informed him.

"And I don't see how running it into here would be feasible," Alex shared.

The king nodded once. "I've had others check into it. They say because of the rock, it would be too difficult."

"I figured as much, which is why I might have come up with a solution." He paused, glancing between the two royals. When no one questioned him, he continued. "What if we have a building dedicated for the servers outside? Demetri's home isn't too far from here, and it has electricity. We could build a place and have electricity run to it, which shouldn't be too hard since they could run it from what Demetri has in place. The building wouldn't have to be immense, just large enough for the servers with room to walk around and fix them."

Varrick rubbed his chin thoughtfully. "What kind

of money are we talking?"

"Depends. You have some pretty handy people here." Alex took in the room with a sweep of his arm. "If all you needed to pay for were building materials and the cost of the electric company running the wiring from the grid, it might not be too bad."

Varrick's eyes darted around the room before landing on his wife. She seemed enamored by the idea.

"Please, Varrick," she pleaded. "I really want us to have computers. That is one of the few things I miss from living among other humans."

The king patted his mate's hand and grinned. Sheesh, if even a demon could find love why couldn't he?

His thoughts turned to Juliette's sister. Maybe that's why he got all hot and bothered around Shira. He just needed a woman, the right woman, to focus his attention on. He should call Samantha before too much longer. With luck, he'd find some time to do so after dinner.

"If you want the internet, Elizabeth, you shall have it."

Varrick's gaze met his. "Make it happen, vampire. I'll fund the building project."

Alex smiled. "You won't be sorry. I really think it is the best solution."

"Since you are already sitting, why don't you eat with us tonight?" Elizabeth offered with a grin. "That way you can fill Varrick and me in on the details."

Alex glanced over at Shira and Dom who appeared in deep conversation. "I'd enjoy that."

While the three of them finished their meal, they discussed his plans for bringing technology to the compound. As he took his last bite of apple, Shira rose, emptied her tray in the closest garbage can, then headed for the door.

Alex stood. "Well, it's been a pleasure dining with you guys, but I'm burning moonlight. I have things which need my attention." *Like a phone call to a supermodel.*

"We'll have to do this again, sometime," Elizabeth graciously offered.

Alex didn't miss the way her mate squeezed her hand after the suggestion. He'd bet Varrick preferred to be alone with his woman, and Alex didn't blame him. If he ever got lucky enough to find a mate, he'd want to keep her all to himself as well.

Alex's gaze fell on Shira. She waited for him by the door, leaning against the wall with her arms crossed under her breasts.

"Looks like I'm in trouble," Alex muttered.

"Perhaps it is because you didn't join her for dinner," Varrick volunteered. "Maybe next time you should sit with her."

The tone of the king's voice made the comment more of an order than a suggestion. *Note taken,* Alex thought, before turning his attention back to Elizabeth. "It was a pleasure dining with you both this evening."

"Bye, Alex." The queen flashed him a bright smile.

"Bye, guys."

Alex crossed the room, his easy strides taking him to the pretty demon leaning against the wall. "Waiting for little ol' me, Shira?"

"You know I am. I'm stuck with you, remember?"

He braced his weight against the wall, his hand resting next to her shoulder. "You know, I can take care of myself. I don't need a sitter."

"Well, obviously some people don't agree."

"And who might those people be?" As if he didn't know.

Shira's full lips pulled into a straight line. He almost expected her to make the juvenile show of buttoning her lips with her hand.

Instead, she pushed away from the wall. "Let's go."

"Where are we going?"

When she didn't reply, Alex followed her down the hall, watching the torchlight play over her pale skin and platinum hair. He ruminated on her beauty when they entered her room. Alex stopped directly inside the doorway and stared.

Unlike his room, her bedroom was rather spacious. A fireplace, built into one wall, beckoned people to come sit on the plush couch across from it. With identical end tables framing the couch and a matching recliner, the room boasted a homey feel. Her large, four-poster bed stood across the room with enough throw pillows to outfit a motel.

His gaze took in the walls. Minerals running through the rock gave the space multicolored stripes which coordinated with the upholstery and bedspread. Around the room, framed pictures hung of Shira with a small child. The boy seemed familiar, but Alex couldn't quite place him.

Shira moved to the sofa, and Alex's eyes fell on the table butted up against the back. Underneath lay a pile of toys, mostly cars and spaceships. Alex's mind clicked the final puzzle piece into place.

His gaze swept between the toys and the pictures

on the wall. Shira was a mother! No wonder she was always so cautious around him.

About to go sit down on the couch, a knock at the door stayed his feet.

"Who is it?" Shira called out.

"Ellie," a female voice responded.

Shira leapt to her feet and bolted for the door.

"Tyler's asking for you, and you said anytime…"

Yanking open the door, she said, "I know what I said."

"Who's Tyler?" Alex asked.

"No one," Shira threw over her shoulder before turning back to the young lady standing in the threshold. "I'll be there in a minute."

"Okay, I'll let him know."

Shira opened the door wider and stood to the side while Alex watched the younger demon leave. "You need to leave, Alex."

Their eyes met. "I thought you were supposed to babysit me."

She blew out a heavy sigh. "Guess you'll have to be on your own tonight. Can you behave yourself?"

When an image of a certain supermodel popped into his mind, he grinned. "I believe I can find something to do to entertain myself."

Suspicion narrowed Shira's eyes. "That's what I'm afraid of." A sigh of exasperation pushed through her lips. "Just stay out of trouble."

****

Jara flinched when The Source placed his hand on her shoulder. The monster scared the Hell out of her. They'd been holed up in this place for weeks, and she couldn't stand the dank, dark cave one second longer.

*Then let's go out and get some fresh air. I'd like a bite to eat,* Eldrick sent over their mindlink.

Always in her mind, the vampire read all her thoughts. The hand on her shoulder tightened until she bowed from the pressure. His strength increased daily.

*Why don't we go into the city, Eldrick? Beijing has much to offer. I could get a real meal instead of the scraps I've been living off. I'm starving.*

*I've noticed you are wasting away.*

Jara's stomach growled in agreement. *So, can we go then?*

*I suppose a trip into the city wouldn't be a bad idea. We need a few supplies.*

Hope blossomed for the first time since being abducted.

*And new clothes,* Jara added. She pulled her dress away from her body. *This has gotten filthy from crawling around this cave.*

Eldrick stood as best he could in the confined space, grabbed Jara's hand, and led her from the cave. Once outside, the full moon shone down on them, casting its silvery glow over the vampire who stood wearing only a pair of jeans she'd stolen one night from their closest neighbor.

His physique had improved much. Broad shoulders now led to defined muscles on his back and chest. Apparently feeding from her helped him regain much of what had been lost during his stasis.

*See those twinkling lights off in the distance, Eldrick? That's Beijing.*

*Are those lanterns burning so high in the air?*

*No, those are lights in the skyscrapers.*

*What is a skyscraper?*

*That's right, you've missed the advancements in the past few centuries.*

A rifling sensation brushed over her mind. Images of the last three hundred years flickered before her eyes. Horse-drawn carriages, the model T, electricity, wars, New York City, the San Francisco Bridge, one modern marvel after another passed in a blur, making her dizzy. Eldrick grabbed her arm when she swayed.

*So much has happened. I must see these things for myself.*

*Can we please start with Beijing? I want real food and clean clothes.*

He gave her an assessing glare. *You* are *dirty.*

She wanted to reply, 'you are too' but refrained, not wanting to anger him.

*Wise decision,* Eldrick commented on the link.

Jara flinched. She really needed to learn how to censor her thoughts.

*Another wise decision.* Eldrick lifted her up over his shoulder and took off through the countryside at a blurring speed.

In seconds, they covered the distance to the city. Standing on the outskirts of Beijing, Jara took in the traffic whizzing by on the road, six lanes deep. The red glow of the brake lights and the white of the headlights mixed with the bluish-white light from the surrounding buildings. Though not as tall as the high rises in New York, the buildings lining the street on either side were none the less impressive.

The promise of a good meal and clean clothes spurred her forward. Eldrick fell into step beside her. His stringy black hair swayed across his shoulders as they walked. Many people brushed them on the packed sidewalks.

*Is it always so crowded?* Eldrick asked.

*I don't know. I've never been here before. You are the one who brought us to China remember? Demons would never live in this place. Too many people, too many germs.*

A familiar tingle went through her mind.

*Ahhh, so you can die from the simplest virus.*

Her irritation increased at the mental invasion, and Jara quickened the pace of her strides. *Do you want me dead, Eldrick?*

*Not yet. I have plans for you. I believe you can help me.*

*You grow stronger every day. You have incredible powers. How can I possibly help you?*

*When the time comes, I'll tell you. Until then...*

Eldrick pulled from her mind, and Jara experienced a moment of relief until he grabbed the nearest human and headed down an alley. The man struggled fruitlessly against the vampire's hold.

Jara watched in horror as Eldrick used one arm to hold the man to him and the other hand to wrench the man's head to the side. A glint of fang flashed seconds before Eldrick fastened his lips to the man's neck. As the blood dripped down the man's flesh, the sound of his strangled scream mixed with Eldrick's sucking. Jara's stomach rolled.

Her hand flew to her mouth, and she turned away from the disgusting sight. When she heard something hit the ground with a muffled smack, she risked a peek and discovered the man lay in a heap on the asphalt with the vampire looming over him.

Breath left Eldrick's lungs in short, hard spurts.

"More." Eldrick's eyes locked with hers.

Panic flooded her veins, made her tremble. He'd been draining her a little at a time for days. Each painful time seared into her memory. "You have a whole buffet out there." Jara gestured toward the oblivious humans walking in front of the opening to the alley. "Enjoy."

The monster's gaze locked on something behind her. She glanced over her shoulder and noticed a young woman walked in their direction. Her sightless eyes appeared glazed as she sauntered up to Eldrick and bared her neck to him. Repeating his earlier performance, he drank his fill, then left her on the alley floor. Five more victims and The Source finally seemed sated.

The odor of blood filled Jara's nose. She retched. Eldrick turned toward her.

*You need to feed as well.*

*I'll take regular food, if it is all the same to you.*

Eldrick's chuckle came across the mindlink. *I assumed as much. Let us find some new clothing then we will go to…What is it called now…A restaurant?*

Jara noticed the swagger in his walk. Power emanated from him, pulsated over her when he neared.

Grabbing her elbow, he pulled her from the alley and down the street.

"We'll need money," Jara announced.

The tingling sensation in her brain returned and a picture of an ATM popped to mind.

*Explain how this money machine works,* commanded Eldrick.

*You stick a card in, type in your pin number and out comes the money.*

*Do they run on battery or electricity?*

*Electricity.*

*Money simply comes out?*

*If you have any in your bank account.*

*Do you?*

*Do I what?*

*Do you have any money in your account?*

*Well, yes, but…*

*Then we need to find one of those machines.*

*Hey! Why must we withdraw my money?*

*Who said we were going to take your money?*

Three blocks later they happened upon a machine.

*Go ahead stick in the card,* Eldrick demanded.

*I don't have my card. It's not like I have a purse or wallet since you kidnapped me.*

Eldrick ran a thoughtful hand down his face and concentrated on the machine. He laid an open hand over the keypad and closed his eyes. A few seconds later, money spit from the machine.

Amazement widened Jara's eyes. "How did you do that?"

He smiled, appearing almost handsome. *Apparently, I cannot only manipulate the impulses of minds but also machines. Actually, the two are very similar. Do you think we have enough?*

Jara gathered the money from the ground and quickly counted it. *I believe so. I really don't know for sure. It seems like a lot, but what do you have in mind?*

She hoped it would be enough for some new clothes, a hot meal, and if she talked Eldrick into it, a hotel room.

*Revenge for Sergei's death among other things.*

Jara glanced from the money in her hands to the

vampire. *Then we'll need more, but I'm sure there are lots of machines in the city.*

## Chapter 7

Talia knocked on the door to her sister's room.

"Who is it?" her twin called from inside.

"Someone who is much prettier than you." Talia smiled wide when Shira opened the door.

"Hard to be prettier when we are identical," Shira quipped as Talia brushed past her.

"Mommy!" Tyler ran to her.

Talia scooped the child up in her arms. "Hi, cutie." She tussled his platinum hair. "Miss me?"

His arms latched tightly around her neck, and he snuggled against her. "Yes, but Aunt Shira played with me."

Talia's gaze met her sister's. The love Shira had for Tyler brought another grin to her face. She lowered the boy to the floor, and he took off for the pile of toys on the bed.

"Want to sit and chat for a while?" Shira offered.

"I thought you'd never ask. It's been a long day."

Talia gratefully sank onto Shira's couch.

"The daycare surprised me when they asked me to get Tyler. Didn't you have today off?"

"I was supposed to, but Bathin was ill, so they called me in to help." She kicked off her shoes and drew her legs beneath her. "The laundry doesn't clean itself, you know. So, tell me about your day."

Shira sighed heavily. "Tiring is the best word to

describe it. That damned vampire."

Talia's eyes widened. "What about him?"

"He's a pain in the ass. He got away from me tonight."

Concern tightened Talia's throat. "King Varrick will not be happy you let the vampire out of your sight."

"I know." Shira rung her hands in her lap. "I found him in the garage."

"What was he doing in there?"

"Working on one of the trucks." Shira's brows rose wistfully, and her eyes drifted toward the ceiling.

"Why are you looking like that?"

Their gazes locked. "Like what?"

A lopsided grin claimed Talia's mouth, and she raised one eyebrow. "Like you are remembering something desirable."

"I have no idea what you are talking about."

When Shira's eyes fell to her hands, Talia realized there must be more to the story. "Oh, yes you do. Something happened." Shira's face reddened. "Dish. I want particulars."

"Nothing happened."

"Tell me, Shira. I want to know. If you don't tell me, I'll make up all sorts of torrid details."

Shira shrugged. "It was nothing. We kissed, that's all."

Excitement straightened Talia's spine. "I knew it! I knew Dom liked you. It was simply a matter of time before you two got together." She patted her sister's knee. "Good for you."

"It wasn't Dom," Shira squeaked out.

Shock widened Talia's eyes. "Really? Who was it

then? Oh, was it his helper Matthias? Or maybe that sexy Lucian, he's a real beefcake."

Shira shook her head.

"Well, who? You have to tell me, sis."

"It was..." Her voice trailed off, and she glanced back at Tyler playing on her bed.

Talia lowered her voice. "He's oblivious. Tyler always is when he's playing with trains. Now tell me who kissed you."

"It was Alex."

"The *vampire*?" Talia voiced the question much louder than she'd intended.

Tyler's head snapped in their direction, and Shira shushed her.

"Yes. Okay? The vampire kissed me. But it didn't mean anything."

A blush took Shira's cheeks, and Talia couldn't help but wonder what caused the color, embarrassment or excitement from remembering the kiss. "Was he good?"

"Talia!" Shira smacked her leg hard.

"Well, was he? I bet he's a great kisser. A stud like that would have had lots of practice." She shifted on the couch then gave her sister an imploring look. "Come on, Shira, you have to share. Since I lost Ose, I live vicariously through your love life now."

Shira took her hand. "You've grieved his loss for years, Talia. It's okay to move on."

Talia nodded her head. "And one day I might. In the meantime, let's get back to you and your sexy vampire boyfriend."

Shira jerked her hand away. "Alex is not my boyfriend."

Talia smiled. "But you can't deny he's sexy."

"Well, yeah. But that doesn't mean anything. Lots of males are sexy, doesn't mean I'm going to jump into bed with them."

"But you need a good romp, Shira. It's been years since you've had a boyfriend. Why not see where things go with the vampire? It's not like you have to marry the guy, just enjoy a little time between the sheets."

Shira's eyes widened. "Sleep with a vampire? I'd sooner bleed myself dry."

Talia rolled her eyes. "Don't be so dramatic. He might be fantastic in bed. You'll never know until you try."

"Talia!" Shira's eyes flew to Tyler then back to Talia before she quieted her voice. "I'm *not* sleeping with the vampire, and that's that."

"Fine, but you have to admit you've been in quite a dry spell in the lover department."

Shira's gaping mouth snapped shut. "Well yeah, but Mr. Right hasn't come along yet."

"Oh honey, you don't need Mr. Right, you simply need Mr. Right Now." Talia wagged her eyebrows.

"Well, I don't see either of them beating down my door, do you?"

Talia patted her sister's hand. "Don't worry, if humans can get a man on the moon, we can get a man on you."

Shira blew out a loud raspberry which made Tyler laugh then run over.

"Mommy, Mommy look what I did."

Tyler lifted the airplane and displayed the decorations he'd colored on it.

"That's beautiful, sweetie. You didn't color on

Aunt Shira's bed, did you?"

He shook his head vigorously, sending his soft curls around his tiny face. "I only colored the plane."

"Let me see," Shira leaned forward and took the plastic aircraft. "Wow. You did a great job, Tyler. Very pretty."

Tyler shifted his weight from foot to foot. "I bet it will fly better now."

"Do you want to try it out?" Talia asked.

"Can I, Mommy? Can I?"

Talia slipped on her shoes and stood while Shira handed the plane back to Tyler. "Sure. We'll take it outside where you can have lots of room for it to fly."

Tyler jumped up and down. "Yay!"

Talia grabbed his free hand, and as they moved to the door said, "But only a few flights, because it is late and a little demon I know needs to get to bed soon."

"Ah, Mommy."

Shira opened the door. "Don't push it, Tyler. You're lucky Mommy is willing to let you stay up this late."

Talia appreciated the backup. It had been hard raising Tyler as a single parent. She didn't know what she would do without her sister, but she'd gladly give up the support if Shira found a male to be happy with and love.

Talia gave her sister a hug. "Thank you."

"For what?"

"For everything." Tyler skipped out the door, leaving Talia no choice but to follow quickly before he got out of sight.

She trailed slightly behind her son. He navigated the halls like an expert, and the pair headed out one of the openings.

The crisp air outside brought the heavy scent of pine. Talia crossed her arms and rubbed her biceps while Tyler launched his jet into the air. He seemed oblivious to the chill. She'd give him five minutes then they'd go in, so he didn't catch a cold. She couldn't take losing him. He was her only child, the love of her life, and life without him wouldn't be worth living.

His delighted squeal drew her from her somber musing. A smile raised the corners of her lips when her son raced after the plane. It soared high in the air, gliding effortlessly through the trees. She ran after him to keep him in sight.

Tyler plucked the toy from the rock on which it landed. "Did you see that, Mommy?"

The precious joy on his face made her grin larger. "Yes, sweetie. I did. It went really far. Why don't you throw it back toward the mountain?"

Tyler turned and threw it in the opposite direction from which she'd suggested. Talia shook her head at her obstinate child. She followed when he ran after it, but the sound of a deep voice slowed her feet.

"Well, yeah. I understand but—"

Talia walked around the nearest tree and discovered the blond vampire. Her eyes followed his form in the moonlight, starting with the thick legs encased in jeans. His back formed a V from his narrow waist to his broad shoulders. She swallowed her lust when she noticed the way his bicep bunched under the formfitting sweater he wore as he shifted his arm to switch something from one ear to the other.

"So how about next week sometime?" His voice held a hopeful note. "Oh, busy then too, huh? Okay."

Alex kicked a rock with his booted foot. "Listen, if you aren't interested in going out, just say so. You don't have to pretend you are busy every time I call." He sauntered forward a couple of steps and plucked a small stick from the ground. His movements were fluid, poetry in motion.

"Well, okay then, don't worry. I won't *bother* you anymore. Goodbye, Samantha."

He jammed the phone into his pocket and hurled the stick.

"Mommy!" Tyler ran toward her.

Her attention fell on her son for a moment. When her gaze returned to the vampire, he walked with a confident stride, exuding power and strength. As he arrived in front of her, she noted the handsome features of his strong face. No wonder her sister had kissed him, she was a fool for not doing more with this hunk of male.

"What are you doing out here, Shira?" he asked. "Did you come to check up on me?"

"I…" About to admit her true identity, Talia quickly decided it might be more interesting to play along. Perhaps she'd hook her sister up yet.

"Mommy!" Tyler tugged on her pants.

*So much for playing along*, she thought as she gazed down. "Yes, sweetie?"

"My plane has a booboo."

Alex reached out a large hand. "May I see it?"

"Can you fix it?" Tyler asked with a pleading voice.

The vampire grinned at the boy. "Well, let's see." He gave the toy a good perusal. "It simply needs a little adjustment."

Alex made quick work of fixing the jet's bent wing and handed it back to Tyler. "There you go, sport. Good as new."

"Thank you." Tyler squealed, then turned and threw the plane with all his might.

Talia gave Alex a smile. "Thank you."

He returned the grin. "Welcome, Shira. You have a great boy there."

Wait! He still thought she was her sister. Talia's grin grew. Hope blossomed.

"So, Alex, who were you talking to?"

"No one."

"Didn't sound like no one."

His foot kicked at the ground, endearing him to Talia. "It really isn't something I'd like to discuss."

"Perhaps I might help." She laid her hand on his arm. The muscles twitched deliciously under the pads of her fingers.

"I don't think there is any helping, but thanks for the offer, darlin'. Of course, if you'd like to do something to take my mind off my troubles." He wagged his light eyebrows at her.

Talia's lips pursed at the double entendre. He seemed flirty and fun. Exactly what her sister needed, but Shira would never agree to go out with him, unless… "I have an idea. Why don't we take Tyler out tomorrow night?"

A smile lit Alex's face. "You asking me out on a date?"

She giggled. "You might call it that, I guess, as much as it could be with a four-year-old tagging along."

"Sounds like fun. Where shall we go?"

"I didn't think that far ahead."

Alex's laugh rumbled deeply from his chest. "Well, since you were polite enough to ask, I'll tell you what. How about we take the munchkin to…what is his name by the way?"

"Tyler."

"Here, Mommy," Tyler called out in response to hearing his name.

Talia's heart leapt to her throat when her attention returned to her child. Halfway to heaven up a pine tree, the thinned trunk swayed under Tyler's weight when he turned back around and reached for the plane. Terror ran cold through her blood.

"Tyler!" she screamed. "Stay right there. I'm coming for you."

But she didn't need to budge. In a flash of movement, Alex scaled the tree. Within seconds, he landed back safely on the ground, the boy in one arm and the plane in the opposite hand.

"You shouldn't scare your mama like that, Tyler," Alex admonished the child. "You cudda gotten hurt."

Talia pulled her son from Alex's arms. "You scared the life out of me, Tyler. You know better than to climb so high. Something might have happened to you."

She nuzzled his head against her shoulder, willing her heart to stop racing, so she could breathe.

Tyler pushed against her, trying to lean back, but she held tight. If anything happened to her son, she'd never forgive herself. Luckily, Alex had been there to save him.

Her eyes met Alex's baby blues. The concern on his face humbled her. "He's all right, Shira. No harm. You can ease up on the hug, you're squishing the boy."

Talia laughed, as much from nerves as from relief. "Sorry, Tyler."

She eased her grip, and Tyler leaned back from her chest. "It's time we all go inside."

Alex shook his head. "You two go ahead. I have another phone call to make, and my phone doesn't get any reception inside the compound."

"We'll wait for you," Talia offered. "Or you can use my phone. It works inside."

"That's okay. I'm not sure how long the call will take. It's a nice night. I don't mind staying out here. You guys go ahead."

"Well, if you're sure." Talia turned and headed for the mountain, Tyler still in her arms.

"Oh, Shira?" Talia stopped and turned toward Alex. "I'll pick you both up at sunset. I have the perfect place in mind for our playdate."

"Okay. I'll see you then, Alex."

The sound of his voice stopped her from walking away. "Oh and, Shira?"

"Yes?"

"I can't wait to play with you." Alex winked.

Holy Hell, that made butterflies flutter in her stomach. Shira would have fun with that male. *If* she'd play.

## Chapter 8

Elizabeth rolled over in bed, and her hand discovered an empty pillow beside her. She sat up and scanned the room. Light from the fireplace danced along the rock walls, creating gray shadows. She brushed the hair from her eyes and pulled back the covers. As soon as her feet hit the floor, she moved to the armoire to retrieve a golden robe with a red, fluffy lapel.

After cinching the scarlet cord around her waist, she checked the bath to make sure her mate was not inside. The boa-like feathers tickled her neck while she made her way back through the bedroom and opened the door.

“My queen,” greeted the sentry stationed outside.

“Hi, Caden. Where’s Varrick?”

“He said he did not wish to be disturbed.”

“That’s nice, but he wasn’t talking about me. Where is he?”

“He gave me instructions to remain here and keep you safe.”

Elizabeth eyed the large demon. With his thick neck and arms, the king’s go-to guy appeared quite intimidating. Normally, Varrick kept the male close, and Elizabeth wondered what he was protecting her from.

“Well, you can remain here, if you want, but I’m

leaving. So, if you want to keep me safe, you better come with me."

With that, Elizabeth closed the chamber door and maneuvered past the guard. The large male marched behind her as she proceeded through the hallway. His booted feet easily caught up to her small strides.

"Where are you going?"

"To find Varrick. Mind telling me where he is?" When Caden didn't reply she continued. "Look, big guy, you might as well tell me where Varrick is, or we'll be walking these halls all night. I won't give up until I find him."

A heavy sigh blew from his wide chest, and Elizabeth couldn't help but appreciate the way his tight T-shirt stretched across his defined muscles.

"I know you won't," he mumbled.

Elizabeth waited silently, knowing she'd get what she wanted.

"King Varrick is in the Tome Room."

A big smile reached Elizabeth's ears. "Thank you, Caden." She turned down the next hall, heading for the sacred room.

"Do me a favor, my queen."

"What's that?" Her steps quickened.

"When the king asks you who told you where to find him—"

She raised her hand, stopping him mid-sentence. "No worries, Caden. You never told me a thing."

A handsome smile reached his red eyes.

When they arrived at the room, Caden reached forward, turned the knob on the massive mahogany door, and pushed it open with one hand. It squeaked on its hinges, announcing her entry.

Elizabeth's eyes roamed the room, seeking her mate. The round room contained walls of rock like the rest of the compound. Stacks of books framed the space, some taller than Varrick, all taller than Elizabeth. In the middle of the room, a three-tiered fountain stood. Fire flowed over the tiers. It sent reddish-orange light flickering around the room, illuminating the way.

Near the fountain stood a podium upon which the Book of Prophesy rested. Varrick stood stoically behind the stand, his shoulders hunched as he read over the pages while Elizabeth made her way to his side.

The king's hand automatically found hers, and he let a contented sigh pass through his lips before his gaze rested on her face. "Hello, my tiny mate." He flashed her a tired grin.

She squeezed his hand. "Hello, my fierce king. You appear weary."

Elizabeth perused his high cheekbones and sensual lips. He boasted a lion's cast to his face, but it didn't detract from his handsomeness in the least. She stood on her tiptoes and brushed a light aureate lock away from Varrick's eyes. Her hand cupped the perpetual five o'clock shadow on his strong jaw.

Varrick's hand covered hers on his face before he spoke. "I am weary, little one." He bent and placed a soft kiss on her forehead as their hands dropped from his jaw.

"Come back to bed, Varrick."

He shook his head. "Not until I find the answer."

"What answer?"

"I need to learn how to destroy The Source. I'm sure the answer is in one of these tomes." He took in the grand expanse of the space with a sweep of his arm.

“How will you ever find it in here? There must be hundreds of books.”

Varrick nodded. “More than a thousand.”

Her eyes widened incredulously. “Do you plan on reading every one?”

“Some I can dismiss, for I know they won’t have the information I seek.”

Elizabeth glanced around the room before her gaze rested back on the king. “Why not let me help you?”

“You don’t know most of the languages in which these stories are written. A few of these were written in demonic hieroglyphs, others in Ancient Sumerian and Latin. Whatever language was common for the day, is the language found in the book.”

“You read all these languages?”

“Yes, I learned them as part of my training to be king.”

“Surely, a few are written in English.”

Varrick smiled, exposing his exceptionally long canines. “A few. Yes.”

“Then let me read those,” Elizabeth offered. “Let me take some of this burden from you.”

Varrick dropped her hand and patted the Book of Prophesy. The scent of musty papyrus and decay accosted her nose. She fought a sneeze.

“I appreciate your generous offer to ease my burden, Little Bits, but I do not require assistance. I am the king, and as such, I will find the answers we need.”

“But I am the queen, and as such I shall help our great king with his quest.”

Varrick chuckled at her formality, for he knew her well enough to realize it was an act, a way to remind him not to be so pompous. Elizabeth giggled and raised an eyebrow as if daring him to continue to dismiss her offer of help.

He tucked her under his shoulder. “Okay, Elizabeth, okay. You win. Let’s see if we can find one of the books in English.”

Two hours later, they exited the Tome Room, each with a book under an arm. As the couple strolled down the halls hand in hand, they came upon their vampiric house guest.

Alex flashed them a big grin. “Well, hi there, y’all.”

“Hello, Alex. What brings you out so late?” Elizabeth asked.

Varrick’s grip tightened around her hand as if to warn her from speaking, but she didn’t care. There was no reason why she shouldn’t be friendly to the vampire. He’d been nothing but nice so far, and at last report, Shira had informed them he’d been behaving himself, so as far as Elizabeth was concerned, he was okay.

“Hello, Elizabeth.” Alex’s eyes moved from her to her mate, and he nodded respectfully when he addressed Varrick. “Hello, Varrick. I was just heading back to my room. What brings the two of you out at this time of night?”

“Actually, it is early morning, vampire.” Varrick corrected rather coldly. Elizabeth squeezed his hand in censure.

“Varrick,” she admonished quietly.

“That’s okay, he’s right. It is early morning, I stand corrected. So, what do you guys have there? Books?”

“A little light reading.” Varrick’s statement made Alex laugh.

“Yeah, right. Those are the biggest books I’ve ever

seen."

"We're looking for a way to end The Source," Elizabeth volunteered.

Alex's blond eyebrow shot up. "And the answer is in those books?"

Varrick glanced around the empty hall. "Since no one is around, I will tell you. I believe my ancestors, the ones who put The Source in stasis, wrote down how they did it. I'm hoping they also mentioned how to destroy the monster."

Alex whistled low. "So, you're thinkin' if you can find where they recorded what they did to Sergei's sire, then you might also find out how to get rid of him."

"Yes," Varrick stated simply. "Now if you'll excuse us."

"Can I help?" Alex reached a hand toward Varrick's book.

Varrick jerked away. "I don't think so, vampire."

"But I thought I was here to help coordinate efforts, help find a way to take out The Source?" Alex stared expectantly at Varrick.

"If we find anything, we will tell you. Come, Elizabeth," Varrick commanded, steering her by the arm around Alex.

****

Jara stared at Eldrick. He lay on one of the beds in their hotel room. His legs crossed at the ankles, fingers threaded together over his stomach. With his eyes closed, he appeared asleep, but Jara wasn't fooled. He was awake. She sensed it.

Every time he forced her to take more of his blood, their link grew stronger. Somehow, she inferred when he was upset or happy, angry or elated. And right now, hunger ruled him.

Eldrick's eyes snapped open, locking with hers. *Come here,* he commanded through their mindlink.

*Please, Eldrick, let me find someone to appease your appetite. If I give you much more of my blood, I'll pass out.*

*Come here. Do not make me force your compliance.*

Jara's feet dragged through the plush carpeting. She wilted under his intense stare. Her eyes roamed the space, wanting to avoid contact with the only other person in the room and desperate to think of anything other than what would come.

They'd rented a suite at a posh hotel. She supposed in any other circumstance she'd have been rather impressed with the place. A large bedroom with two double beds and a desk, a kitchen area, and giant bath. The amenities were plush, the decor top of the line. But the fear running through Jara far outweighed any excitement at finally being about to sleep in a real bed after weeks of sleeping in that damned cave.

Her eyes passed briefly over the pile of money on one of the beds. They'd hit every ATM they found downtown and now possessed enough currency to last them a month, even with paying for this place.

*We won't be here that long,* Eldrick informed her.

She crawled onto the bed and laid down beside him. *Why not? What do you have planned?*

His bloodlust washed over her when he spoke. *I plan on gathering my followers and making a run at taking out the Alpha Council.*

He bit into his wrist. *Take, drink. My blood will make you strong. You are right. I've taken too much from you lately.*

Jara pulled away. She didn't want more of the monster's blood. She hated drinking from him. The coppery aroma made her nose tingle, her mouth salivate. She shook her head no. She didn't want it. Didn't want him. She didn't.

But the fragrance acted like an aphrodisiac. It called to her. She watched it bubble up on his flesh, run in twin lines down his arm.

*Drink.* Eldrick moved the temptation closer to her mouth.

Instinct took over, and she latched onto the arm, gulping the blood down as fast as it flowed. Jara's tongue lapped at the thick, coppery substance. It burned like acid down her throat. Every cell in her body seemed to be on fire, but she couldn't stop drinking.

He pulled away. *That's enough, Jara. No more.*

Jara rolled onto her side, back to her captor. Her breath sawed from her lungs in heavy puffs. Her vision swam before becoming acuter. Eldrick's heartbeat pounded in her ears, and she wondered how that was possible. She smelled his unique scent, and under that, she caught the whiff of carpet freshener the maid must have used. Jara's skin registered not only her clothes and the sheets that touched them but the air itself.

What the heck happened? It was like all her senses fired at once.

Eldrick chuckled. *I'll tell you what is happening, Jara. You have become addicted to my blood. You crave it. It makes you more than you normally are. It makes you stronger, better.*

Oh, Goddess help her! He was right.

## Chapter 9

Bright blue energy coalesced in Shira's hand. She lobbed the fireball into the hearth. The flames crackled as their reflections danced around the room. The warmth bathed her in a fiery glow which felt good after the long day she'd had.

Shira noted the time and blew out a hard sigh. Unfortunately, it would no doubt be a long night. Duty called. She straightened her red pantsuit, brushing her hands down her thighs.

Why did she bother to do so? It's not as if she cared how the vampire thought she looked. She glanced at her reflection in the mirror above the dresser.

"Really, I don't care," she assured herself before three knocks pounded on the door.

"Bet I know who this is." Shock made her brows rise when she opened the door wide. "Talia?"

Her nephew ran past her. "And Tyler. What a nice surprise, but unfortunately, I don't have much time to visit. I need to get to my assigned duty."

"Your assignment will come to you," Talia informed her.

Shira shook her head. "No, he won't. Alex never seeks me out."

"He will tonight." Talia affected a Cheshire-cat grin.

Suspicion narrowed Shira's eyes. "What aren't you

telling me?"

"I never could keep anything from you." Talia's attention turned to Tyler. "Don't jump on Aunt Shira's bed, darling. You'll get hurt."

"Oh, Mommy," Tyler's exasperated whimper made Shira chuckle. "I'm being careful."

"Get down, son. Why don't you play with your toys?"

Tyler landed on his bottom and bounced off the bed.

Once he'd chosen a toy, Shira continued, "Being a twin has its advantages. One of which is knowing what the other is up to. Spill it, sister dear. Why do you think the vampire will seek me out tonight?"

Talia took a deep breath and gave a forced smile. "Okay. Don't be mad, but I kind of set you up on a date tonight?"

Her stomach lurched. She didn't. She wouldn't! "You *what*?"

Her sister had the decency to appear contrite. "Last night Tyler and I were in the forest. We came across Alex. One thing led to another and…well…I kind of pretended to be you, and now you and Alex have a date."

Anger mixed with trepidation, and Shira paced in front of the fireplace. On multiple occasions over the years, she and Talia had masqueraded as one another. But never had Talia done something like this.

Shira rounded on Talia, hands fisted on her hips. "I can't go on a date with the bloodsucker. I'm supposed to be *guarding* him."

"Seems like you could do both." Talia settled on the couch and rested one arm on the back of the thing, appearing carefree.

Of course, she was carefree. She wasn't the one who had a date with a vampire.

Talia wore a catty grin. "Why not go out with Alex? He said he knew exactly where to take you."

Shira joined her on the sofa. "I have no intention of being alone with Alex."

"You won't be alone. Tyler is coming too."

Now that's a twist she hadn't expected. "Tyler will be there?"

Talia nodded. "You should see Alex with him. They were quite sweet."

She just bet they were. Alex probably tried to ingratiate himself by being nice to Tyler.

"I don't care how sweet Alex is, I'm not going."

The last thing she needed was to like the bloodsucker. Being attracted to him was one thing. After all, what woman wouldn't appreciate that body and handsome face? But liking him, dating him, now that was something else entirely. Even if her feelings toward him had been growing of late, she had no intention of fostering anything between them.

"Methinks the demon doth protest too much." A knowing expression graced Talia's face.

"I protest because I don't want to go on a date with the vampire."

"I didn't want to do this, but you've left me no choice. If you don't go, I'll be forced to go in your place."

Shira's eyes widened. "You wouldn't dare."

Talia pursed her lips and tapped a thoughtful finger on her chin. "I'll not let the poor guy be stood up. If you won't go, then I'll attend for you. Hmmmm, I wonder what I might do with him. Wonder what we might talk about."

It wasn't an empty threat. Her sister loved causing mischief. If Talia impersonated her, there was no telling what she might do.

Butterflies circled in Shira's stomach. "Fine. You leave me no choice. I'll go out with the vampire."

Talia smiled a toothy grin. "I knew you would."

"I'm only going because you are making me."

Talia nodded. "Sure, tell yourself that, if it makes you feel better."

She *was* only going because of Talia. She didn't want to date Alex. Really, she didn't. Perhaps if he were a demon, but he's a vampire, and she didn't like vampires. Well, maybe she liked one, but she didn't want to fall in love with him.

As if reading her thoughts, Talia said, "Look you don't have to fall in love with Alex. Go. Have a good time. Watch how he is with Tyler. A lot can be learned from watching how someone interacts with children."

*That's true.*

A knock sounded.

"There he is. Have fun."

Shira crossed the room and opened the door. Alex stood on the other side, dressed in a pair of black jeans. They molded to his thick thighs and led to a white button-down shirt. The fabric stretched over his broad chest. Rolled-up sleeves showed his muscular forearms. Her gaze traveled to his strong jawline, over his perfect nose, and landed on the aquamarine eyes that crinkled when he smiled.

Alex tipped his head. "Hello."

The man oozed sex appeal. Maybe tonight

wouldn't be so bad after all. Shira's heart fluttered. "Hi."

"Ready to go?"

"Sure, let me get my purse."

When Shira moved around Tyler playing and went for the bag, Alex stepped into the room. "Don't forget Ty…what the heck?"

Talia stood. "Hello."

Alex's brows rose in shock. "You…two…" his gaze flew back and forth between the women. "You're twins?"

Shira smirked. "How very observant. Alex, this is my sister, Talia."

The vampire rounded the couch to shake Talia's hand. "Nice to meet ya."

"Likewise."

Poor guy. Alex appeared terribly confused. She almost felt sorry for him.

Almost.

"Talia, I'm not sure when we will be back."

"Don't rush on my account. Go. Have fun."

Tyler jumped up. "We go now?"

Shira smiled. "Yes, cutie. We are going."

"Where are we going?"

Shira shrugged. "Ask Alex."

Tyler gazed up at the vampire with expectant eyes. "Where are we going, Alex?"

The man smiled, appearing relaxed for the first time since knocking. "I have a surprise for you. I think you're going to love it."

"Yay!" Tyler jumped up and down. "I love surprises."

After a short car ride into the city, the three sat at a

table in Cool Town. While Alex and Tyler ate, Shira took in the place. The building held everything a child might dream of wanting. A roller rink, an arcade, and a laser tag arena sat on one side, while the other half consisted of an indoor playground, complete with climbing tunnels and a ball pit. Children ran amuck while parents chatted.

Alex cleared his throat, garnering her attention. "So, Tyler, what do you want to do after we finish dinner?"

Tyler wiggled in his chair. "The playground."

Shira chuckled at the child's exuberance. "Looks like he can't wait."

"Why should he have to?" Alex asked. "Tyler do you want to go play and finish your hotdog later?"

Tyler nodded his head with such enthusiasm, his hair danced around his scalp. "Can I?"

Alex glanced at Shira. "Depends on what your mother says."

"Aunt Shira isn't my mommy."

Alex's brows popped up, touching his bangs. "But I thought he is yours. The pictures in your room. The toys by your bed."

Shira shook her head. "Talia is his mother. I keep the toys around, so he'll have something to do when he visits. He needs to keep busy."

Tyler stood, shifting from foot to foot. "Can I go?"

Shira laughed. "Yes, cutie, you can go."

Her watchful gaze tracked Tyler as he ran to the playground and climbed into a plastic tube. Shira took a bite of her hamburger and chewed it slowly, allowing her time to think.

The vampire thought Tyler was her son. Would he

treat the child differently, knowing he was actually her nephew? Would Alex continue to be interested in the boy and entertain him as he had on the way to Cool Town? Time would tell.

Alex bit off a chunk of hotdog and swallowed before he spoke. "I hope you don't mind me bringing us here. On a first date, I usually choose a place with less noise."

Shira took a sip of her soda. "It's fine. Tyler is loving it."

"I noticed he got super excited."

"That's because he's always wanted to come here."

"He's never been here before?"

"No."

"Why not?"

Talia had kept him away in the past. She didn't want to risk Tyler being exposed to the germs. Shira understood why, but one look at his tiny face when they'd pulled into the parking lot, and Shira couldn't deny the child entry.

"Talia is afraid he'll get sick."

"That's ridiculous. We'll make sure he washes his hands before he eats."

Obviously, Alex didn't know about the demons' issues with their immune system, and it wasn't her place to tell him. Varrick had made it clear the less he knew about them the better.

Shira rifled through her purse and found the hand sanitizer. She placed the container on the table and squirted a dollop into her hands. "Don't worry. I have it covered."

Alex's lips closed around the straw in his drink. Shira followed the movement of his Adam's apple bobbing with each swallow. His tongue darted out to lick that delectable mouth when he finished.

Alex seemed to notice her perusal for he leaned forward. “The saying ‘look but don’t touch,’ doesn’t apply to you. You can touch all you want.”

Memories of their previous kiss came to mind. Temptation pushed Shira forward. Apparently, her body would love another round of kiss-me-baby.

Her gaze fell to those full lips. A warmth pooled in her tummy. Her lips puckered in invitation.

Through hooded eyes, she observed Alex lean closer.

Suddenly, he cocked his head. “Do you hear that?”

His head snapped toward the playground.

“Hear what?”

“It’s Tyler. He’s upset.”

Before Shira asked how he knew that, Alex stood and marched quick-time to the playground. He squeezed into a tube as Shira made her way to the area. By the time she arrived, he’d shimmied up to the landing where Tyler sat.

The two spoke, and Alex pulled Tyler into his lap. The large male sat hunched around the child, cradling him in his arms. Suddenly, Tyler laughed. Alex replied in kind, and the two scampered down the slide.

“What was all that about?” Shira asked as they arrived by her side.

Alex placed a large hand on Tyler’s shoulder. “Just a boy thing. Right, Tyler?”

Tyler flashed Alex a huge grin. “Yeah. A boy thing. It’s okay now.”

“Ready to finish your dinner?” Shira asked.

“No,” Tyler squealed and dashed for the ball pit.

He dove in headfirst, disappeared under the balls, then popped up and waved to the couple.

"So, what happened?" Shira asked when Tyler was out of earshot.

"He couldn't figure out how to get out."

"So, you showed him?"

"First, I told him everyone gets stuck sometimes, and when you do, you need to take a breath, calm down, and laugh."

One eyebrow rose on Shira's face. "Laugh?"

Alex gave an insouciant shrug. "I figured if I got him laughin' then he'd calm down."

"It seemed to work. Did he reason how to get to the slide, or did you help him?"

"He did it all by himself. He's a great kid," Alex commented.

Shira laughed. "Butt."

"No buts about it." Alex put a hand in the pocket of his jeans. "He's great."

Shira shook her head. "No, not but, butt. B-U-T-T." Shira pointed at Tyler and laughed.

Alex joined in when he glanced at the boy and witnessed the child mooning them.

"Kiss my butt, Alex," Tyler taunted, wiggling his pale bottom.

"I'll get you for that." Alex took off for the pit.

Tyler squeaked, pulled up his pants, and dove under the balls.

Alex plowed into the sea of plastic. He surfaced near Tyler. "You deserve a good tickling for that little stunt."

Tyler squealed with glee and leapt away. "You can't get me."

Alex disappeared under the multicolored plastic and reappeared in front of Tyler. He jumped in surprise and took off in the opposite direction. The cat-and-mouse game continued for several minutes.

A wisp of black smoke appeared each time Alex vanished under the balls. Shira's eyes narrowed on the emerging pattern. Alex would go under the balls, and they would rise, the balls would settle back down then a puff of smoke appeared before Alex would reemerge in a new spot without disturbing the balls in between the two places.

Her mind worked the puzzle. *He's dematerializing.*

It was the only logical conclusion. She'd have to inform Varrick of this news when they returned. For now, she'd put duty aside and enjoy the fun.

Shira's heart sang with joy at the sight of the two playing. Each time Alex materialized near Tyler, he'd scream and run the opposite direction. Finally, Alex made good on his promise and tickled Tyler mercilessly.

"Stop. Stop! I'm gonna pee," Tyler cried.

Alex immediately grabbed him under the arms, and the two made a quick exit from the ball pit.

As they whizzed past Shira, Alex called out, "We'll be right back. Need to make a pit stop."

Shira sauntered back to the table as her mind replayed the playful session. Likening Alex to a predator was only natural. A male of his physicality could be aggressive and capable of violence. But she was learning there was more to this vampire than his virility. He seemed kind and funny. She was beginning to get comfortable around him, beginning to like him. A warmth wound around Shira's heart. She might be in over her head. If Alex decided to pursue her, would she be able to stall his advances? Did she want to?

Alex led Tyler by the hand back to the table then helped him climb into the chair. As Alex sat, their eyes met, and he gave her a sexy grin. She must admit, he was good with Tyler, and it endeared him to her.

"That was fun," Tyler exclaimed around a mouthful of hotdog.

"Tyler!" Shira's stomach seemed to drop to her toes. She grabbed the sanitizer. "Here use this before you eat."

"We washed up in the bathroom," Alex offered.

Concern creased her brow. "Can't be too careful."

Tyler went back to chowing down on his dog, and Alex leaned back in his chair. "I didn't figure you for a germaphobe?"

"There's a lot you don't know about me."

"I'd like to get to know you, Shira." His blue eyes pinned her with a poignant stare. "If you'll let me."

His sincerity made a warmth spread in her belly.

"I think tonight is a good first start." She smiled.

"I think so too." Alex's shoulders eased, and the sexy grin returned. His hand covered hers and gave it a squeeze. Warm tingles raced through her.

All too soon, he withdrew. "Now, if you don't mind, I have an errand to run since we're in town. Shouldn't take me too long. How about you guys stay here and play while I do what I need to?"

Let him out of her sight to roam the town alone? Not going to happen on her watch.

"Actually, Tyler is looking tired," Shira offered.

"I am not." Tyler popped the last of the hotdog in his tiny mouth.

Shira tussled his platinum locks. "You never think you are tired, but it's getting late. Alex, let's head home, and you can do whatever errands you need to on the way."

Alex appeared conflicted. After a few seconds, he acquiesced, and the trio went to the car. Three blocks later, they parked in front of a construction building.

Alex turned off the vehicle and rotated toward Shira. "Wait here. I'll only be a minute."

When he slipped from the vehicle, Shira waited until he went inside before unfastening her seatbelt and removing Tyler from his car seat. Leading the child by the hand, they entered the building and followed the sound of Alex's voice down the hall.

"I appreciate you staying late to accommodate my schedule," Alex commented as Shira promenaded through the doorway.

A portly gentleman sat behind a small desk while Alex parked his bottom in one of the folding chairs located opposite the man.

"Mind if we join you?" Shira settled herself in the empty chair and pulled Tyler onto her lap.

"Not at all." The foreman reached across the desk and shook Shira's hand. "I'm Burt Connors."

"Nice to meet you. I'm Shira."

Tyler reached out his tiny hand and waited for Burt to shake it. "I'm Tyler."

"Very nice to meet you, Tyler." Burt clasped his hands on the desk. "So, Mr. Hall, what can I do for you?"

"I asked my architect to send over a schematic."

"He did. I looked at it this morning. Seems simple enough."

"It is. I don't need much for a hunting cabin."

"I noticed it doesn't have a bathroom or any pipes for running water, don't you think you'll need those?"

Alex shifted forward, captured the foreman's gaze with his eyes. The man's face dropped, all expression gone.

"The schematic has exactly what is needed. There is no reason to question anything about it. You will build it to specs and not ask any more questions about the project."

"I will not ask any more questions about the project," Burt repeated in a monotone voice.

*So, the vampire can hypnotize people. That's something else Varrick needs to know. He better not have hypnotized me!*

Tyler shifted in her lap, snuggling against her shoulder.

Alex broke contact with the man, and he blinked rapidly, coming out of the mental haze.

The vampire leaned back in the chair. "So how long do you believe the project will take?"

"We aren't very busy right now. Probably three weeks, maybe less."

Alex nodded. "Sounds good. Here is the survey for the land where the cabin will be going. Anything else you need from me tonight?"

"Nothing I can think of. I'll pull the permits, and we'll get started on construction."

"What about a contract?" asked Shira.

"We already have one, ma'am." Burt tapped a folder on the desk.

Alex turned her way. "Varrick took care of the legalities. I'm just doing the grunt work."

"Oh." Shira sat up straighter in surprise, and Tyler stirred against her chest.

Alex smiled. "The little man's asleep. We better get you two home."

Burt stood and reached out an arm. "It's nice to finally meet in person, Mr. Hall and Miss Shira."

Alex shook the man's hand. "I'll be in touch."

Shira stood. "Goodbye."

Alex followed Shira to the car. After she buckled Tyler in the back, he held open the passenger door for her, and she slid into the seat. After Shira confirmed the so-called hunting shack would really house the servers, they rode the remainder of the drive to the mountain in silence.

The quiet gave Shira time to absorb all she'd learned about Alex. He'd been great with Tyler. The two were adorable, and they'd had fun. *She* had fun, and if she were being truthful with herself, she had to admit she'd enjoyed the date.

When they got to the compound, Shira jumped from the vehicle and triggered the secret door. The vine-covered granite opened wide, and Alex pulled into the garage, placing the car in the lineup of vehicles.

They ambled to Shira's room. All the while she wondered if he'd try to kiss her again. Did she want him to? Would she stop him if he did?

Butterflies fluttered in her tummy.

Alex carried the sleeping Tyler in his arms and neither said anything while they wound through the halls, giving her time to imagine all sorts of kissing scenarios. When they arrived at Shira's door, she opened it and turned expectantly toward Alex, having determined a goodnight kiss wouldn't be the worst thing in the world.

Shira's heart beat hard in her chest. "Thank you for a fun time tonight."

Shira licked her lips, and Alex's eyes followed the motion. "I had a good time too. We should do it again sometime."

"Only next time, I pick the place." Her breath came in tiny puffs.

This was it. She could tell by the way he leaned closer. The butterflies turned to ponies, driven into a frenzy by her galloping heart and the fact her palms had decided to sweat.

Alex affected a hurt expression which Shira felt sure he faked. "What, you didn't like Cool Town? How can you not like a place called *Cool* Town? I'm hurt. Really, I am. Maybe you should give me a kiss to make me feel better."

When his sly grin showed his dimple, she giggled. Tyler stirred and kicked Alex squarely in the groin. His face squinched in pain. He handed the child to Shira and bent at the waist with his hand over the injury.

"Like aunt, like nephew," he spit out through clenched teeth.

Shira pursed her lips together to keep from laughing.

Talia joined them. "What's that supposed to mean?"

Shira no longer stopped the laugh. "It means I kicked him in the family jewels too."

"I think I need to lie down." Alex grunted then straightened.

Disappointment settled her stomach. Looked like she wouldn't have to worry about those palms now.

"Can you make it to your room?" Shira asked, though he clearly felt a little better.

"Normally, I'd say something like, maybe you better escort me, but I think I'm better off alone until my groin is back in action."

"I'd bet that would be some good action too," Talia murmured.

Shira blushed, mortified. "Okay, Alex. Good night."

"Good night."

In her haste to close the door before her sister embarrassed her further, Shira slammed the thing.

Tyler snuggled against his mother. "I'll go put him down. Shira, we'll talk tomorrow."

"I'm sure we will."

In fact, it was just as well that she was leaving. Sweaty palms and racing heart aside, duty called. Even though the date hadn't been a total disaster, she stilled needed to report what she'd learned regarding Alex's powers to Varrick. Her loyalty was to her king, not the sexy vampire who made her libido go into overdrive.

Thankful Talia decided to go, Shira opened the door. "Good night."

"Good night, Shira."

Shira peered into the hall. Talia trailed behind Alex. When both were out of sight, she closed the door and headed for the Throne Room, duty foremost on her mind.

## Chapter 10

Eldrick's eyes snapped open, and he rose from the bed in a fluid motion. The demon bitch lay in the next bed, awaiting his command to wake. As he had done on every previous dawn, he'd forced her to sleep to keep her from escaping.

The vampire pulled on slacks then donned a silken shirt. He brushed a hand down one sleeve, appreciating the cool fabric under the pads of his fingers. He had to give the woman one thing; she possessed good taste in clothing.

*Maybe she'll be useful for more than just revenge, after all,* he thought while he buttoned the sleeves.

He chuckled. *As if I'd ever consider keeping her around. She's just a means to an end. Once she's served her purpose, I'll destroy her.*

His gaze fell on her lifeless form. Disdain snarled his upper lip. *Look at her. Small. Weak-minded. She disgusts me. If I was at full strength, I'd snap her in two like the bug she is and go after the Alphas myself. But I can't. Not yet.*

Each time they shared blood they both grew stronger. Jara didn't realize it yet because he'd kept the knowledge from her mind, but she now possessed every power he did. The blood exchange gave her all the same powers as a vampire while allowing her to keep her demonic abilities as well. But he dared not allow her to know it. For if she realized she was damned near as powerful as him, she might get away. And that simply couldn't happen.

As much as Eldrick hated to admit it, he needed her. He had an attack plan, and like it or not, she had a part to play.

*Wake!* he sent the command over their mindlink and remained, as always, in her mind.

Jara's eyes blinked as she struggled through the inky blackness of sleep.

*Get dressed, demon. We must leave.*

*Where are we going?*

*Siberia.*

*What? Why?*

*You dare to question your master?* Over the link, Eldrick sent the sensation of fire throughout her body. Jara screamed.

*Stop! Please, I beg you. I'm sorry.*

Eldrick halted the pain. *Get dressed we leave in ten minutes.*

Jara crawled from the bed, her muscles aching from the punishment. The sight brought a smile to his face, the likes of which would have made the devil cringe.

As she donned jeans, she kept her gaze subverted. *May I eat before we leave?*

*No. There's no time. We need to get there before they have a chance to rise.*

*They who?*

*Stupid twit. The Alphas. We are going back to Siberia to finish what we started.*

Jara blanched and pushed her arm through the sweater. *How do you know they are still there? It's been weeks.*

Eldrick sent another wave of fire over the demon. She collapsed on the floor, writhing on the carpet.

*Any more questions?*

"Nooooo," she screamed.

He ended the pain and sent her an image of where he wanted to go. *Materialize here immediately. And if you aren't there when I coalesce there, I will hunt you down, and the pain you just suffered will be nothing compared to what I will do to you.*

Fear widened her eyes. She dematerialized. The smell of sulfur reached his nose as he scattered his atoms.

His form coalesced by the frozen river. His gaze immediately located Jara. *Smart demon.* At least he wouldn't have to track her down.

His eyes scanned the barren landscape, landing on the tunnel from which he'd emerged from the stasis the demons placed him in centuries ago.

Anger boiled in his blood. His hands fisted at his sides. Once the Alphas were dealt with, the demons were next on his kill list.

*So now what? What is your plan?*

*We kill the Alphas. We will divide and conquer. Once we locate them, we'll attack on two fronts. You'll draw some and finish them off while I dispose of the others.*

*That's suicide. They bested us last time. Why would it be any different now?*

Eldrick marched to Jara with purposeful strides. Anger brought his hand down hard on her cheek. The demon's head jerked to the side, and she stumbled from the force of the blow.

*You dare to question me? Me! Do you honestly doubt my power after the past days with me? Have you not sensed your strength growing?*

He ran a hand through his black hair, pulling it away from his face. *Surely, you can feel my blood coursing through your veins. It strengthens you. You can fight. I've seen you. Help me destroy the Alphas, and I'll set you free.*

Of course, he didn't expect her to survive the fight. She was fodder, nothing more, but if luck was with them, she might just take one or two of the vampires with her.

A handprint formed, cherry red, on her cheek as she tucked platinum strands behind her ears. *I have your word?*

Eldrick nodded.

*Then show me your plan.*

Eldrick sent the battle plan over their mindlink. Its simplicity would be why it would work. While he goaded the Alphas into assaulting him, she would come up behind the combat and attack. When some of the Alphas engaged her, she'd back away, drawing them from Eldrick.

The vampire kept the rest of the plan to himself. With luck, two of the Alphas would engage the demon bitch, leaving him with five. He could easily defeat five vampires. After which, he'd finish off the other two and the demon, assuming they hadn't already done so.

*Now, come here for one last blood exchange, then we attack.*

Jara approached Eldrick. He scored her wrist with his fangs, then did the same on his arm. They brought the other's wounds to their lips and drank simultaneously. After a few minutes, both healed.

When they dropped arms, Jara rubbed where the wounds had been and gazed up at him with wonder. “How is that possible? My wounds healed so quickly.”

*I told you that you were stronger. My blood has given you gifts. Use them wisely.*

*What else has your blood done?*

*It increased your speed. You can heal.*

*What? I can heal? Drinking your blood heals me?*

*Yes.* Irritation grated his nerves. He didn’t have time to school her. They needed to find the Alphas.

*So, if I get sick, all I have to do is drink your blood, and I won’t die.*

*You won’t get sick as long as my blood runs through you.* Not that it mattered since she wouldn’t be living much longer.

Elation forced a smile that reached her red eyes. Eldrick didn’t trust the expression and easily read her intentions in her mind. Apparently, her kind had been looking for a way to harness the vampires’ immunity to disease as well as their ability to heal. The idiots had not thought it could be as simple as consuming the vampire’s blood. She intended to inform her brother of the discovery as soon as he let her go. Which, of course, wouldn’t happen.

*Jara, concentrate. I need you to focus. We go into battle.*

Eldrick stalked through the forest on silent feet. Jara followed behind like a good little sycophant should.

*When we find them, you’ll disappear. Wait until I have their full attention, then attack.*

*I understand.*

They came to an A-frame house. Eldrick climbed onto the porch and peered through the windows. Empty! He roared his ire. It shook the tiny home on its foundation, rattling the windows.

Jara shrank back.

*There are not here.*

*Maybe they are out feeding,* she feebly offered.

Eldrick sent his senses flaring over the landscape and found no one. He scanned the frozen land with his eyes. His preternatural eyesight zeroed in on movement. A tiger stalked across the fallen snow, its white coat blending seamlessly with the barren forest of Larch trees.

It pushed through the tree line and locked eyes with him. The beast's claws dug into the ground before it sprang in their direction. A single leap brought the mighty beast onto the porch. Jara's scream echoed in the night as he grabbed the cat's throat.

Man and beast landed in a heap. The beast straddled him. Large teeth gnashed at his face. Its hot breath ghosted over his skin with each lunge. Only the hand around the tiger's neck held it at bay.

Eldrick dematerialized. He reformed on its back as the cat bit into the porch. Eldrick wrenched its head until the flesh gave and ripped from its body with a tearing sound. The tiger collapsed on the porch. Eldrick tossed the head over the rail.

His breath slowed in time with his heartbeat, and he turned toward Jara. She stood motionless, her gaze on the head rolling slightly back and forth by her feet.

*I've seen a lot of fighting, but I've never seen anything like that. It ended before the tiger even had a chance.*

*That is how our fight with the Alphas will be.*

She glanced at him. *Do you really think so?*

*I have no doubt.* Confidence straightened his spine. *But we must find them first.*

*I could scry for them.*

Eldrick pulled the process from her mind. In doing so, he noted the location she'd been in at the time. *You found them in Savannah.*

*Yes. They seem to have a nest there.*

*There's no time to waste while you acquire the implements to scry. We will go to Savannah and look for them there.*

*What if we can't find them?*

*Then we will hunker down for the evening, you can scry for their location, and we'll attack tomorrow. One way or another, we destroy the Alphas soon.*

****

Varrick sat on the velvety throne, working his sword with a sharpening stone. The sound of metal scraping rock echoed in the room. The steady rhythm focused his mind. He'd been through most every tome and found nothing of significance. The same could be said of Elizabeth.

Ah, his Elizabeth. A smile pulled his lips. Sweet, kind Elizabeth. The light to his darkness. She made him want to be a better man, and if there was ever a time he needed to be better, it was now.

With The Source awakened, his sister on a killing rampage, and his people still no closer to discovering how to boost their immune systems, they needed a strong leader. A leader who would fight for them, give them hope. Elizabeth made the world brighter. She made him smile when all seemed lost.

His mate looked at the world through optimistic glasses, and it became contagious. Never before had he felt so hopeful about the future. With Elizabeth by his side, the world was his.

Varrick's gaze fell on the empty chair beside him. She waited in their chambers, reading over the tomes, while he held court. He missed her gorgeous face. Missed running his fingers through her silky hair.

He'd been here long enough this evening. It was time to have some private time with his sexy mate. Varrick stood.

The door opened, and in walked Shira wearing a determined expression. Varrick sat.

"Yes?"

Shira bowed. "Forgive me, Sire, but I have news to report."

Varrick placed the sword across the arms of his chair. "By all means, share your tidings."

Shira's eyes were ablaze with excitement. "I have discovered information about the vampire."

His interest piqued, Varrick's eyes widened.

"Well, go ahead," he prompted when she hesitated.

"Alex can dematerialize. Only instead of doing it the way we do, when he does it, it leaves a little wisp of smoke behind. He can hypnotize people too."

"How did you come to learn these things? Did he share them with you?"

"I saw him hypnotize the construction foreman who is building your structure in the forest."

His eyes narrowed on his subject. "You went to town with the vampire?"

Shira's head jerked back, and her eyebrows furrowed over her eyes. "Well, yes."

"Why ever would you take such a risk?"

"We were on a…a…the vampire had errands to run, and I decided to accompany him."

Varrick took a deep inhale. He rested his elbows on the sword and steepled his fingers. "Why do I get the impression you tell falsehoods?"

The petite demon bowed her head. "I do not wish to anger your highness."

"Then tell me the truth. I have charged you with watching the vampire. Did I put my faith in the wrong person?"

Shira shook her head and tucked her white hair behind her ears. "That's what I did tonight. I was watching him. I couldn't allow him to go into the city alone."

Varrick cocked his head as he assessed the statement. "Very well. Anything else to report."

Shira's eyes locked with his. "That is all for tonight."

"Fine. You did well. Continue to keep an eye on him, and in the future, do your best to discourage him from going into town." The king leaned forward until the sword touched his stomach. "Do whatever you need to in order to keep him in the compound."

"I can find a way to keep him occupied."

Her face reddened though Varrick couldn't be sure why. Perhaps she found the vampire enticing. They had a reputation for wooing women. He made a mental note to keep an eye on the situation.

Varrick leaned back against the red padding. "If that is all for this evening, then you may take your leave."

Shira bowed at the waist and backed from the

room. Cyrus reached for the door behind her.

Varrick raised a staying hand. “Hold, Cyrus. I’m leaving. No need to shut the door.”

The king returned the sword to its scabbard and walked through the opening. Cyrus closed the heavy door then fell in behind Varrick. They moved through the dimly lit hall silently.

When they arrived at his chamber door, Varrick turned and addressed the guard, “I thank you for your service this night, but I can take things from here.”

“Don’t you wish for me to remain outside your door?”

Varrick’s plans involved a lot of passionate screams from Elizabeth, and she would be mortified if the guard heard. “I think not tonight. You can go to your chambers. Get some respite.”

Cyrus bowed. “As you wish, Sire.”

Varrick turned the knob and pushed through the door. The sight awaiting him made blood rush to his groin.

Elizabeth lay on their golden couch, dressed only in his T-shirt. It fell loosely down to her knees. She looked like a small child playing dress up. The image brought a smile to his face which softened his eyes.

"I approve of the way you look in my shirt. I think you should wear my clothes often. In fact, I might make it a rule.”

“I don’t do well with rules,” she teased, drawing her knees up under her and shifting the book held in her hands.

“I expect my subjects to obey.” Varrick placed the sword on a table by the door and crossed the room.

“I’m not your subject. I’m your mate. Now sit

down and come see." Excitement gleamed in her eyes, and the smile she flashed him lit the room. "I found something."

Varrick joined her on the couch. His finger traced the ivy pattern around her leg. He gathered her legs in his lap. "What is it, Little Bits?"

"I found a passage about The Source. It didn't say much other than talk about how he has vast powers and can best most any demon."

Varrick massaged her leg. "We knew that."

"True, but here is the kicker. A few pages later, the author wrote, 'To kill the beast, still his beating heart and all will come to a fiery end'."

"That is generic, like a horoscope in a newspaper—anybody could read into it and make it applied to them."

"But what if it applies to The Source?"

"Let's say it does. What exactly does it mean?"

Elizabeth tugged her lower lip between her teeth. "I haven't found out yet, but I'll keep reading."

Varrick pulled the tome from her hands and gently placed it on the floor.

"I think you've done enough reading for this evening." His fingers trailed up her thigh. "I think you need a break."

He kissed her thoroughly as he ran his hand over her body memorizing every curve and swell. Goosebumps pimpled her skin under his touch. He could not help the grin which pulled at the corners of his mouth, forcing him to break their kiss.

Her breath pushed from her lungs in short spirts. "Mmmmm. What did you have in mind?"

In response, his finger found the edge of the tee

and slipped beneath. His hand spanned her leg. His thumb made tiny circles on her inner thigh, stealing her breath. Her body immediately responded to the sinful touch.

Varrick captured her lips, pushing her onto the couch with the weight of his body. Desire circulated between them, increasing with each pass. His tongue swirled lazily around her mouth.

Varrick kissed a trail down her jaw, stopping to nuzzle at the hollow spot where her neck met her shoulder. His tongue traced the mark located there that told the world she belonged to him. He bit, reinforcing his brand in an animalistic way that sent a rush of heat through his body.

Elizabeth rubbed her thighs together as if seeking relief. A low moan pushed through her lips. Her fingers bunched in his hair, giving it a painful tug.

Her body was his playground, and he enjoyed every minute of play. This was how he wanted her, wild, uninhibited, responding to his touch. When he stilled and lifted his head, she panted. She looked beautiful, her eyes glazed with ecstasy.

"Please," she whispered.

"Please what, Elizabeth?"

"Please, I need…I want…" She didn't finish the thought.

"What do you want? Say it," he demanded, still holding her golden eyes with his.

"I-I want you," she stammered.

Varrick rose from the sofa, took her in his arms and carried her to the bed.

"Then you shall have me," he replied before placing her on the mattress.

## Chapter 11

*Alex.*

Alex stilled under the blankets

*Alex, you awake?* Stephan's voice boomed over their mindlink.

Alex rubbed the day sleep from his eyes. *I am now. What's up?*

Alex stretched.

*I want you to come to Marcus' plantation.*

Alarm forced him into a seated position in bed. *Why? Something wrong?*

*I want to hear what you have found out about the demons.*

*There's not much to report. They are very recluse.*

*Be that as it may, Katrina wants you here.*

Now that seemed more than a little strange. *Katrina?*

*Yes. Kitten wants everyone together for Thanksgiving.*

Holy Hades! He'd forgotten about Thanksgiving. Alex fluffed the pillow behind his back.

*How'd that creep up on us?*

Stephan's laughter crossed the link. *That's exactly what Marcus said. Everyone forgot. If it hadn't been for Juliette mentioning it, the holiday would have passed without celebration.*

*There's been too much going on.*

*You can say that again. Now the women are downstairs busy prepping, and each of us have an assigned duty. I've been put in charge of grocery shopping.*

*That should be fun.* A mental image of the Alpha leader traipsing around the local box store with a long list in his hand made Alex smile.

*Oh, it is* great *fun. You should see all the last-minute shoppers. Carts blocking every aisle. Shelves emptied of most of the traditional items. It's like people are prepping for a natural disaster, and I'm stuck in the middle of it.*

*Why not cancel Thanksgiving this year?*

*Nicholai suggested that. Let's just say, the women didn't approve of the idea.*

Stephan sent Alex a memory of Juliette and Katrina rounding on Nicholai, hands on their hips, reading him the riot act. The expression on the poor guy's face almost made Alex feel sorry for him. Almost.

Alex laughed. He'd missed his comrades. They were a great group of males. He could certainly use a little time with them. Not to mention, he didn't want to be the next to earn the women's wrath.

*I'll get dressed and pop right over to the plantation.*

*Wise decision. I'll see you there.*

Stephan left Alex's mind, and he pushed from the bed. He tugged on a flannel shirt then donned a pair of faded jeans. After he ran a comb through his short hair, he brushed his teeth, thankful he'd chosen to get a shower before going to bed. One less thing to do was a blessing.

A knock sounded on the door just as he was about to dematerialize. "Yes?" he called out.

"It's me," Shira hollered through the door.

When Alex opened the wooden door, Shira's eyes gave him an appreciative once-over. Her admiration made one corner of his mouth snake up in a cocky grin. "Come for the goodnight kiss we didn't get to have last night?"

Her eyes widened before her hot gaze fell to his mouth. He licked his lips for effect, and she blushed.

"I…We…uh…no."

Alex forced a casual shrugged, even though the thought of kissing her delectable mouth made his libido stand up and say howdy. "Too bad. I hoped you might be game."

She took a deep breath as if to collect herself. "I stopped by to see if you would help Dom in the garage tonight. During lunch, he asked about you and wondered if you could assist him."

*Why didn't Dom stop by himself?* Alex wondered. Did he dare to hope she'd offered to come instead simply to see him? Dressed in a Grecian-style flowy gown, she appeared like a goddess. A beautiful, wanton goddess.

"I told him I'd come by after you woke to ask you." Shira clasped her hands behind her back.

Alex couldn't help but admire the way the movement pushed her plump breasts out for his perusal in the valley the plunging neckline created. Nice of her to come by herself and give him this tantalizing view.

"I'm glad you came. But I can't help him tonight."

"Why not?"

"I won't be here."

Shock made her delicate eyebrows rise on her forehead. "Where do you think you are going without me?"

"Darlin', as much as I adore spending time with you," Alex moved closer before continuing, "And I do like being with you."

The Alpha bent and whispered the next words in her ear. "I like talking with you. I like teasing you…I like—"

He allowed her imagination to finish the sentence.

Shira's breath sawed from her lungs. "What else do you like doing with me?" she whispered.

Alex straightened and gave her what he hoped was a sexy smile. "This."

His hand cupped the nape of her neck and pulled her to him for a kiss. His lips brushed hers. His tongue darted out to lick the seam of her lips. They opened, inviting him inside. The warm cavern of her mouth tasted like honey. Their tongues danced. Shira pushed her body against his.

Alex's hand snaked around her waist pulling her tightly against him. His body responded immediately. Blood rushed through his veins. Shira's arms wove around his neck.

Suddenly, a tiny voice called, "Aunt Shira, where are you?"

Annnnnd didn't that just suck!

They broke apart just as Tyler came into view, and Alex suppressed the groan trying to force its way out of his throat.

Alex ruffled the boy's platinum locks. "Hey there, big guy. Where'd you come from?"

The child grinned. "From Mommy's room."

Shira brought a hand to her kiss-swollen lips. "Where is your mommy?"

Tyler sneezed. Snot blew from his nose, and before anyone could stop him, he wiped it away with his sleeve.

"Yuck." The corners of Shira's mouth turned down in disgust.

The mood broken, now seemed like a good time for Alex to share his news. "I'll let you go take care of that."

"Leaving the yucky work for me? And just what are you going to do while I'm on snot patrol?"

"As I started to tell you earlier. I have been summoned to Savannah by the leader of the Alpha Council."

Shira's mouth drew into a taunt line as she rested a hand on Tyler's shoulder. "Why?"

"It's Thanksgiving. Everyone is getting together to celebrate." It was as good an excuse as any. Shira didn't need to know he'd be reporting on the demons to Stephan. "Don't demons celebrate Thanksgiving?"

Shira shook her head. "No, but we are aware of the holiday. When will you return?"

Alex gave her a sly grin. "Why? Already miss me?"

Shira crossed her arms under her bosom. "No."

Well, that would have hurt, *if* he didn't believe it was a lie.

Tyler tugged on her gown. "Aunt Shira, I gotta go potty."

The babe wiped his nose along his forearm.

"And you need to blow your nose." Shira placed him on her hip. "Varrick will want to know when to expect your return."

Alex nodded. "I'm not sure. Maybe a day or two. It shouldn't be long. Everything is in good shape. The construction on the server shack should start any day. I've ordered the servers, computers, and plugs. All we need is a place with some electricity and the stuff to come in, then you guys will be digital downloadin' demons."

"Aunt Shira," Tyler whined and wiggled in her arms.

"Okay, Tyler. I guess I better go."

She appeared reluctant to leave, and Alex hoped it might have more to do with missing him then a desperate avoidance of taking Tyler to the bathroom to clean the snotty nose.

"I'll come and find you when I return. Promise." Alex drew a small, imaginary cross on his left pec.

Shira's laugh lightened his heart. "Well, since you crossed your heart, I guess I have no choice but to believe you. I'll hold you to that promise, vampire."

"I'd expect nothing less." The Alpha gave a slight bow of his head.

She turned and headed down the hall.

Alex shut the door and pulled his molecules inward until he dematerialized, leaving only a wisp of smoke behind.

He reformed on the porch of Marcus' plantation home and knocked on one of the front doors. While he waited, his eyes roamed over the white siding and green shutters. Marcus' mate opened the oak door.

"There you are! Come in," Christina's southern accent was music to his Virginian ears.

Alex stepped into the foyer. He'd been in the space

a ton of times, but it was still damned impressive with the crown molding and Mort Kunstler paintings hanging on the walls. Not to mention the huge staircase that wound its way to the second floor.

"Happy fangs-giving," Alex greeted with a large smile.

Christina gave a demure giggle behind her hand. "You're a hoot. We've missed having you around."

"I've missed being here." Alex's stomach growled, and he gave it a rub to settle the beast. "Did I make it in time to eat?"

The French doors on either side of the space were open wide. Marcus emerged from the set on the right. "Always thinking about food, aren't ya, big guy? Well, it'll be a while."

Marcus stopped in his tracks and wrinkled his nose. "What's that stench?"

He sniffed the air then his eyes landed on Alex. "It's you! What the Hell, man?"

Alex rolled his eyes. "I have to use this special soap the demons gave me. Apparently, they have an issue with the way vampires smell."

"So, they prefer you smell like a flower garden?" Marcus teased.

Christina smiled. "Stop it, Marcus. I think he smells good."

"You would, *cara*."

Christina shook her head. "There's nothing wrong with a man smelling nice."

"Just don't go expecting me to start smelling like a rose." When Christina laughed, Marcus clamped a hand hard on Alex's shoulder. "So, how've you been?"

"Just fine. So where is Stephan? He said he wanted

a briefing."

"Our mighty leader isn't back from the store yet."

As if on cue, a car pulled up the gravel drive outside. Marcus opened the door and called out, "Need help?"

Stephan unfolded from the sports car. "I think I should have taken one of your other vehicles, Marcus. This baby is full."

Alex and Marcus bound down the stairs, grabbed several bags from the trunk and left Stephan to retrieve the groceries from the passenger seat.

They walked through the hall and into the large kitchen. Juliette frantically pulled pots and pans from the pan rack above the granite island while Katrina had her head inside a fridge that boasted a faux door which matched the white cabinets on three walls of the space.

"Where should we put these?" Alex lifted the multiple bags hanging from his hands.

Julie squealed. "Yay! We can finally start dinner."

Katrina crossed the kitchen with a tub of butter and patted the island in the center. "Here would be good."

As Alex placed the bags on the granite countertop, Nicholai and Tatiana passed through the entryway from the dining room.

Nicholai crossed to Juliette, tucked her under his arm and gave her a peck on the temple. "It took us half the night, but the table is all set, *lastochka*."

She graced him with a gorgeous smile. "That's wonderful. Thank you, sweetheart. I appreciate the help."

"What else can I do?" Nicholai asked.

Julie dug through the bags and pulled out a package of frozen cranberries. "Turn these into cranberry sauce."

Nicholai took the bag from her hand and bent low at the waist. "Your wish is my command."

"Hi, Alex," Nicholai tossed over his shoulder as he crossed the kitchen. He appropriated a pot from Kat and began to assemble ingredients for the sauce.

"Hi," Alex returned, while Marcus unburdened himself.

Kat gave Alex a hug. A low groan emanated from the doorway as Stephan entered with Christina on his heels.

Alex raised his hands in surrender. "She instigated it, not me."

Kat pulled away and laughed. "Don't worry, Alex, he's all growl and no bite."

Stephan placed the last of the groceries on the island. "I beg to differ, Kitten, I bite you all the time."

He pulled his blonde mate into his arms and nuzzled her neck.

Tatianna shook her head, sending her short black hair shaking around her face, and huffed. "The kitchen is getting crowded. I'm going to join Demetri in the gym and get in a workout before we eat." She glanced at Alex. "Glad you made it."

Alex nodded. "Me too."

Kat pushed away from Stephan. "Actually, Tatianna has a point. You've heard what they say about too many cooks in the kitchen."

Katrina peeked in three bags. She wore a concerned expression when she glanced up at Stephan. "Where's the turkey?"

Juliette's speed increased as she rifled through the remaining bags. "We must have a turkey."

The tiny demon with multi-colored hair, known as Harleigh, entered with Desmond close on her heels. She waved at Alex, and he returned the greeting.

"It won't be Thanksgiving without a turkey!" Christina pushed her fingers through her red hair.

"Don't worry," assured Marcus. "I'm sure Stephan got a bird."

"I did," Stephan informed them, and the group gave a collective sigh. "I got a chicken."

He produced it from one of the bags. "They were out of turkeys."

Kat faced her mate. "You must go back out. There has got to be a turkey somewhere."

Stephan shook his head. "There isn't a turkey in the city. I even went outside of the city limits. No one has a turkey."

"Thanksgiving is ruined," Kat cried.

"Do not cry. My heart cannot take it." Stephan pulled his woman into his arms.

Harleigh cleared her throat. "Sheesh. Don't go off like a frog in a sock."

All eyes fell on the Aussie.

Nicholai's eyebrows rose high on his forehead. "Did you just call Stephan a frog?"

Harleigh laughed. "I said don't go off like a frog in a sock. It means don't go crazy. If it means that much to you, *I'll* go get a turkey."

"You know where to find one?" Alex asked.

Harleigh nodded. "I know where one is. I'll pop there and be back in a few minutes with the thing."

She dematerialized before their eyes, leaving only the smell of sulfur behind.

"See," Stephan pulled slightly back from Katrina.

"Everything will be fine."

Kat smiled and wiped her forehead with the back of her hand, leaving a streak of flour. "Just like always."

"Now, if everything is under control, Alex and I need to have a little chat." Stephan glanced at Alex before returning his attention to Katrina.

"Of course. Go have your chat. We can handle things in here."

Marcus, Stephan, and Alex made their way through the hall to the music room. The space had been transformed. Previously, it contained a grand piano and enough seating to accommodate a large audience. Now padding covered the mirrors which lined the walls. Toys littered the floor. The largest playpen Alex had ever seen stood in the middle of the room. Pacifiers and bottles with red liquid lay strewn over the bottom of the pen.

Alex nodded in the direction of the apparatus. "Been redecorating I see."

Marcus chuckled. "With baby Viktor in the house, certain things needed to be done."

Stephan clasped Marcus on his shoulder. "Decorating is not the only thing the little guy has done."

"What do you mean?"

"Well, the females are all bothered about having babies of their own."

Marcus kneaded his chin. "Christina is dying to have a rug rat. I keep explaining that because she was human it could take centuries, but she wants one something fierce."

Stephan nodded his head. "Kat too. They indicated

they want to have children at the same time."

Alex whistled between his teeth. "As if having one at all wasn't hard enough, they want to time the births."

The Alpha leader shook his head. "I know. It would be impossible."

Alex shrugged. "Miracles can happen, I guess, but it will be hard as Hell to pull off."

"Speaking of Hell, tell me all about the demons."

"Not much to tell. So far, I've explored most of their compound. They assigned a guard to me, but I can usually find some time off by myself to nose around."

"Varrick said nothing of a guard," Stephan mused.

"What's the guy like?" asked Marcus.

"He's a she," Alex informed them. "She's nice. And pretty."

Marcus wagged his brows. "So, you are working the Alpha charm on her, huh?"

Alex smiled. "You might say that."

"Like Desmond is on Harleigh," Stephan added.

"Now there's an interesting development." Alex grinned. "Tell me more."

"First, tell us what you have learned about the demons."

"The compound is huge. Lots of rooms. Their society runs in a definite hierarchy with Varrick at the top. Each person does something in the compound to earn their keep and help the collective."

Stephan nodded and thoughtfully rubbed his chin. "Have you learned how to defeat Eldrick?"

Alex shook his head. "Not yet, but I did stumble across a room full of books. Unfortunately, one of Varrick's guards found me before I got a look inside any of them. I plan on talking Shira into letting me peek around in there once I go back."

"Who's Shira?"

"My personal guard."

"I'll have to speak with Varrick about—" A shriek cut off the remainder of Stephan's statement.

The three males streaked from the room with preternatural speed, arriving in the dining room in time to see Nicholai catch Juliette as she fainted. He rushed her from the area, crossing paths with Natasha who cradled Viktor in her arms.

Vlad followed his family into the room. "What the devil? You woke the baby."

Harleigh held a large white turkey by its neck. The bird beat its wings.

Feathers floated in the air as Kat spoke, "Where in the Hell did you get a live turkey?"

"What's wrong with a live turkey?" Desmond inquired in his cultured tone before moving next to Harleigh to assist her in wrangling the bird.

"I saw a story about him on TV," Harleigh offered.

"You mean that's the turkey we saw on the news?" Natasha's voice rose in astonishment. "Tell me that's *not* the same bird!"

Harleigh faced her friend and shrugged. "They weren't going to use it. The reporter said they'd pardoned it."

"Pardoned it?" Stephan repeated and approached the petite demon with anger in his eyes. "You didn't. You wouldn't! Is that the *presidential* turkey?"

Desmond stepped between them. The turkey started a new round of flapping. "Calm down. The president wasn't going to eat it. We saw no reason for it to go to waste."

*Damn!* Leave it to an Aussie and a Brit to not understand the significance of stealing Tom the Turkey from the White House.

Stephan's power filled the room. Baby Viktor cried when it prickled over their skin. A blue aura surrounded Harleigh when she gathered energy in response.

The bird produced a strangled gobble noise and fought like a kickboxer in an MMA ring to escape. White feathers filled the air. Its legs kicked wildly, and its body jerked from Harleigh's hand.

Tom landed on the dining room table and made a run for it. Cups of blood spilled over the fine china and silverware flew from the table like missiles. Baby Viktor leapt from his mother's arms and landed on the bird's back. He wrapped his little arms around the skinny neck as his legs straddled the bird.

Vlad threw himself headfirst down the table to grab the boy, but Viktor must have decided he was hungry because he bit the fowl's neck. The bite acted like spurs on a horse, and Tom put on a burst of speed. Vlad's fingers brushed its tail, but the warrior missed the bird.

"Get them!" Natasha screamed.

Viktor released his bite and gave a contented squeal then giggled. The turkey continued its run down the long table, Viktor riding it like a ranch hand. Each Alpha, in turn, made a play for the bird as it passed.

*That sucker is fast*, thought Alex.

He materialized at the end of the table and crouched in a defensive stance. Like a linebacker, he grabbed the bird around its middle and plucked Viktor from its back. The turkey under one arm and the baby in the other, he grinned while everyone cheered.

Natasha ran to him and pulled her child from his

arm.

"Bad baby," she scolded. "Don't you ever scare Mommy like that again."

When Tom gobbled, Viktor reached for the bird.

Alex moved away. "I think you've had enough time with the turkey for tonight, little one."

He locked eyes with Stephan. "What should we do with this thing?"

Their leader's eyes narrowed on Desmond and Harleigh. "These two are going to take it back and hope they don't get caught."

Something occurred to Alex. "How did they get the thing here? Vampires can't dematerialize with another live thing."

Desmond straightened slightly and placed an arm proudly around Harleigh's shoulders. "But demons can."

A collective gasp sounded in the room.

Hours later, Tom had been safely returned, the table reset, and the group sat enjoying their chicken dinner with all the trimmings.

Alex glanced around the table.

Vlad fed Viktor, so Natasha could eat. "Are you sure you don't want to eat? I could feed Viktor," offered Natasha.

"M*ilenky*, you eat. I can wait." Viktor scooped up a handful of peas and reared back. Vladimir's large hand encompassed his immediately. "No, young one. There will be none of that."

"He's growing so quickly," commented Christina.

Natasha smiled and nodded. "That's what vampire babies do. They grow much faster than humans, aging at about a year in only four months. By the time they are a year old, they look and act like a preschooler."

Julie's eyes widened. "Wow. Nicholai told me once I become a vampire, I'll stop aging. What about Viktor? If he ages so rapidly, won't he grow old?"

Nicholai covered Julie's hand with his own then gave it a squeeze. "The accelerated growth only lasts about two years, just long enough to give the little one a chance to defend itself, then the child ages normally for a while. Viktor will stop aging around thirty or so and remain that way forever."

"How about baby demons, Harleigh?" Natasha glanced the demon's way over her next forkful. "How do they age?"

"They age at the same rate as humans."

Desmond placed his arm on the back of her chair. "Do they stop aging?"

Harleigh nodded. "As long as they live long enough, the aging slows around age twenty-five. We still age, but very slowly."

"What do you mean by 'live long enough'?" asked Stephan.

Kat reached over and squeezed his thigh. "Not tonight. It's a holiday. Let's not interrogate anyone at the table."

"Isn't that a tradition at the Thanksgiving table?" Marcus' quip earned him an elbow in the ribs from Christina. By the way she giggled, Alex realized the jab came from a place of good-natured ribbing. Pun intended.

All the team appeared happy, relaxed. Each gazed on their mate with love in their eyes. Alex experienced a moment of jealousy.

Shira came to mind. He missed her. Missed the

way she made him work for every kiss. Missed her smile. His chest tightened. Fates help him, but he'd developed feelings for the woman.

She'd been with him so often the past weeks, he hadn't noticed, but being without her tonight, especially while surrounded by all the couples, made him realize he cared for her. He couldn't wait to get back to the compound and see her.

"Are they rebuilding First Bite, Marcus?" Tatianna's question provided a much-needed distraction.

"I heard they are moving it to another city," Christina offered.

Tatianna's brows furrowed. "Why?"

"Because after what happened, vampires are leaving the area in droves, *kotik kisa*," Demetri informed the group.

Katrina tsked. "That's a shame. Maybe someone should buy the business and keep it here."

"How about your sister, Julie?" Marcus suggested. "She has lots of money."

Just what Alex needed, to see Sami again. He barely kept his eyes from rolling.

Juliette shook her head. "I don't think she'd buy it. She's too busy planning her wedding."

"What?" Alex didn't keep the incredulousness from his voice.

"She told me last night. She was on a photo shoot and met a guy in Paris. He's the head of some fashion house. It is a match made in heaven, according to her."

Well, that explained why she wouldn't go out with him. No big loss. He wished her a happy life.

"I think we may have another match in heaven,"

Marcus tipped his glass toward Desmond.

Alex's gaze fell on Desmond and Harleigh sneaking a kiss. Stephan cleared his throat. When the pair separated, he spoke.

"I guess congratulations are in order."

Harleigh smiled. "Yes."

"How long?"

Desmond rested his arm around Harleigh's shoulders. "A few days."

Stephan pursed his lips. "Do not exchange blood."

"Stephan!" Kat's outrage resonated in her tone.

Their leader waved off the reprimand. "I want it clear from the start I do not believe vampires and demons should exchange blood. We don't know what might happen."

Anger reddened Desmond's face. "No one has exchanged anything, but who are you to make such an edict?"

"I'm the leader of the Alphas," Stephan proclaimed.

Apparently, Harleigh didn't care for the declaration. Her red eyes glowed. Sparks of electricity bounced from her fingertips. "You aren't *my* leader."

"I am while you are living under this roof."

Holy Hades them was fightin' words.

"Maybe I should leave then," Harleigh challenged.

Desmond paled and placed a supportive hand on her forearm.

"I'll speak to Varrick," Stephan offered.

Desmond stood. "This really guts me. Stop!"

Everyone turned their attention on DW. Alex admitted the vamp had balls to take on Stephan and a woman. Maybe he should help the fella out. Alex opened his mouth to speak, but Harleigh stood.

"I'm done. Let's go, Des."

Des? There was a new nickname.

"Don't go," Julie cried.

Desmond forced a smile. "Thanks for a lovely meal, but we'll take our leave if it's all the same. Meet me outside, love."

With that the couple both dematerialized.

Silence fell over the group.

"Well, we've always said we are like a family," Marcus commented.

Demetri cleared his throat. "I think we proved that tonight. We certainly experienced a Thanksgiving full of traditional drama."

"That's been our way of life lately," Tatianna reminded them.

"Unfortunately, I don't expect things to get better anytime soon," Stephan chimed in.

## Chapter 12

*Find them now!* Eldrick's voice boomed in Jara's head. She flinched, expecting any moment to be set ablaze.

*I need to concentrate, and it isn't easy with you hovering.*

Eldrick crossed the room and placed his hands on the table at which she sat. They bordered the map of Savanah stretched across the wooden surface.

*Find them,* he repeated. His dark, intense stare sent a shiver of fear up her spine. *I will kill someone tonight. It can be you as easily as one of them.*

Jara's hand tightened around the stone it held. Her skin tingled at its touch, and its magic flowed through her veins. She stared at the map. It blurred as she focused her inner mind on the Alphas.

Her hair hovered away from her scalp, and a blue aura bathed her in an ethereal glow. Centimeter by centimeter, she moved her hand over the map.

The ice-cold scrying stone began to warm. With great restraint, Jara continued to move her hand slowly. The stone's warmth increased until it seared her flesh.

Her hand shook with the effort to contain the stone. It became translucent. Its crystalline beauty a sight to behold as the scintillation of the stone burned brightly in the dim room. The odor of smoldering flesh accosted her nose, turned her gut. Its stench grew in direct correlation to the white-hot sting in her palm, but she forced it all aside as her eyes flew to the map to note the location over which her hand hovered.

"There," she gritted out through teeth clenched in agony.

She allowed the stone to drop from her hand, pulling some of her flesh with it as it fell. A hiss escaped her ruby lips. Her finger tapped a street.

*Are they all there?* Eldrick's irritation crossed the mindlink.

*I'm not sure. Let me check.*

While the stone returned to its original color, she retrieved the bowl of water from the table. Jara cupped the bowl between the palms of her hands and bent over the container, concentrating on the water within. She took several deep, cleansing breaths, forcing the pain away to concentrate properly.

The water spun counterclockwise, swirling until a blurry image began to form. Like a specimen in a microscope, the image in the water cleared, showing Jara the ones she sought.

At first, she spied a gravel drive lined with oak trees. The Spanish moss hung in droves, creating an eerie sight. The driveway led to a white, plantation-style home. Like a panoramic shot on a movie screen, the image narrowed until the surrounding trees were lost from view and only a house remained.

Her magic pushed through the door to the home. Inside she heard boisterous chatting. She followed it into a dining room. There the Alphas sat eating.

Eldrick's fist pounded on the table, making the water shimmy in the bowl. *Tell me what you see, now!*

She pulled her mind from the image and swayed.

Jara's hands grabbed the edge of the table for support. Her arms shook from the effort.

*They are in a mansion. All of them are together, even their mates.*

*All the better. We'll take their mates from them before I kill them. It will add to their suffering.*

*If we attack them together, how will we be able to make sure the females are killed first?* asked Jara.

A sanguine smile took his face.

*I will pull the males away from the home. You will hunt and kill the females while I keep their mates occupied.*

*But some of the women are vampires. How can I go up against multiple vampires?*

*You have my power within you.*

*What?* Jara didn't still her features in time to keep the disbelief from her face. She hoped it didn't earn her punishment.

*It came from the blood exchanges. You are nearly as powerful as I am.*

*I can do everything you can? I can hypnotize people?*

*Of course, you and I share powers. Use my gift to end the Alpha's mates, and once I end the Alphas, the world will be ours.*

Another shiver traveled through her body, but this time it was pure anticipation at the thought of ruling the world. With Eldrick by her side, not even her brother could stop them. They'd rule over demon, vampire, and humans alike. She'd once again rule, as she was born to do. Only this time it would be the entire world!

Greed changed her expression into a derisive smile.

Eldrick's chuckle crossed the link. *Now your feeble*

*mind is beginning to understand.*

*What are we waiting for?* Jara stood. *Let's go.*

****

Juliette put the final glass in the dishwasher, closed the door, and started the wash cycle.

"That was a fast clean up," she remarked with a smile.

Natasha nodded her head. "It helps when most of us have vampiric speed."

Christina laughed. "It sure does. Speaking of which, when are you going to convert, Julie?"

"I don't know. Nicholai isn't pushing me to go through it until I'm ready."

"The conversion process is a bitch." Katrina's eyes darted to Julie. "But it's totally worth it."

Christina moved to the island. "I agree. I love being a vampire."

"I'll do it one day," Julie promised. "I honestly don't know why I'm so hesitant."

Natasha laid a hand on her shoulder. "I'd imagine it would be a little scary. Thinking about going through all that pain. I liken it to childbirth. I was petrified to give birth, but I knew it would be worth the pain. For the record, I was right. Viktor is worth every second."

Julie smiled up at her sister-in-law. "Viktor is adorable. I hope Nicholai and I can have children one day."

"I'm sure you will," Natasha assured her. "In the meantime, appreciate the time you have as a couple, because once a baby comes along, you rarely get a minute for yourselves."

Christina ran water over a dishrag and wiped the countertop. "Sounds like someone needs a little alone time with her mate."

"I wouldn't turn down the opportunity."

An idea came to Juliette. "Why don't you and Vlad go out. I'll watch Viktor."

"We couldn't." Natasha waved off the offer. "You worked so hard tonight getting the Thanksgiving feast made. You must be exhausted."

"I'm not tired at all. I drank two cups of coffee with dessert," Julie shared. "Plus, I'll have help, right ladies."

Kat and Christina nodded.

"We'd love to watch the baby," Christina said.

A large grin spread from ear to ear on Natasha's face. "It would be a good night to get out. I'm sure most humans are tucked into their beds by now after eating those big meals."

"Then it's settled." Julie clapped her hands. "Go tell Vlad you are taking him out on the town."

Thirty minutes later, Julie sat with Christina and Kat in the living room. Viktor hobbled between them and collapsed in Julie's lap. She offered him the toy bird she'd been holding.

"Are you sure we should let him play with that?" asked Christina. "Maybe that's why he attacked the turkey.

The women laughed.

"That was hysterical!" Kat pulled her blonde hair back into a ponytail and secured it with a hairband.

"Did you see the look on Vlad's face when he jumped on it?" Christina laughed harder.

Julie picked up the baby and turned him toward

her. "You gave Daddy a big scare tonight. Didn't you?"

Viktor smiled.

Kat pointed at the boy. "Look, he thinks it's funny."

"I think Natasha and Vlad are going to have their hands full," commented Christina.

A malodorous odor wafted on the air. "I don't think he's smiling because he thought daddy was funny." Julie held the baby from her. "I think he was going number two."

Christina clamped her nose between her finger and thumb. "Yew!"

Kat covered her mouth and nose with her hand. "This would be one of those rare times it is bad to be a vampire. Super smell isn't a good thing around a dirty diaper."

Julie rose with Viktor in her arms. "I'll take care of this."

"Thank you," came the chorus from the grateful vamps as she ascended the stairs.

When she arrived at the top, Nicholai materialized in front of her. His concern flowed over their mindlink, twisting Julie's stomach.

"I must go." His voice sounded grave.

"What happened?"

"Natasha just contacted me through our mindlink. She said she and Vlad were walking around Forsyth Park when they spotted Eldrick and Jara."

Panic gripped her heart. "Are they all right?"

Nicholai nodded. "Yes. They hid, but—"

Panic contorted his face. His fear for his sister flooded her mind. Viktor must have sensed the unease for he began to cry.

"What is it?" Julie bounced Viktor.

"They've been spotted. Vlad informed Stephan. We must go help them."

Julie's heart raced. "Absolutely, go."

Nicholai leaned down and gave her a quick peck on the lips. "I love you, *lastochka*."

"I love you too." Julie grabbed his arm and waited for their eyes to lock before she continued. "Promise me you'll come home to me."

He pulled her hand from his arm and kissed the back of it. "I promise."

Alex blurred by them then dematerialized by the front door bypassing the stairs.

"That is my clue. I must go."

Julie smiled. She loved it when he mispronounced the idiosyncrasies of the English language. "You mean that's your cue."

Nicholai flashed her the grin she found so sexy. "Yes. My cue."

"Go. We'll be here when you return."

Nicholai dematerialized, and smoke wafted in the air.

The smile dropped from her face. He better return. Julie knew he could take care of himself. He'd been doing this sort of thing for centuries, but tonight felt different. Dread clamped around her stomach, and her meal threatened to make a reappearance.

Viktor stopped crying and kicked his legs, drawing her attention.

"Okay, little one. I know. We need to clean you up."

Once in the nursery, Julie laid him on the changing table. Christina had done a great job decorating the place before Natasha's family moved in. The light-yellow walls boasted sayings in calligraphy about happiness and family. The crib, dresser, toy chest, and diaper table were all made of the finest wood. But tonight, even the cheery décor couldn't distract her from her unease.

She changed Viktor with the quick efficiency of a mother and memories of her girls pushed in on her. She had loved everything about them as babies, even changing the diapers. And there were a lot of diapers since they were twins.

Viktor let out a howl, and Julie cradled him against her chest. "What is it, sweetie?"

She bounced the babe and headed out the door. As she reached the top of the stairs, the crying got worse. "What is the matter? Are you hungry?"

At the foot of the stairs, Kat and Christina came out of the living room to see what caused the commotion.

"What's up with him?" Christina asked.

"It's almost like he's sensing something," Kat offered.

The women glanced around.

"I don't sense anything," Christina said.

"Neither do I," Kat replied.

"Maybe he's hungry," Julie suggested.

"That's probably it," Katrina agreed. "Christina and I thought we would go down to the TV room and watch a romcom. You game, Julie?"

"Sounds like a great idea. Let me get some blood from the fridge for the little man, and I'll meet you down there. Do either of you want a bag?"

Christina patted her stomach. "I'm still full from dinner."

"Me too." Kat poked out her normally flat tummy and gave it a rub.

"All right. You go pick out a good movie, and I'll be there by the time the opening credits roll."

As the women headed downstairs, Julie and Viktor went into the kitchen. After she retrieved a bag of blood, they moved down the hall toward the basement.

The front doors groaned, and Julie's gaze darted to the foyer just as they tore from their hinges. In the next second, all Hell broke loose. The wood splintered into a thousand pieces and flew their direction.

Julie turned, shielding Viktor. Shards embedded in her back. She screamed. Viktor cried. When the wood settled on the floor, she turned back to the opening.

A woman advanced. Her platinum hair pulsed from her head. A blue aura flooded the room with light. Sparks, actual sparks, flew from her fingertips. Her red eyes glowed bright, and the snarl she wore on her lips showed teeth. Power flowed over them.

The hair on Julie's body stood at attention. Viktor released a blood-curdling scream. Kat pushed the basement door open, and Julie noticed Christina on her heels. The demon's eyes moved to the women. They glowed a fiery red, filled with intensity and concentration.

"Stop!" she commanded.

They froze mid-stride. Terror seized Julie's gut.

"Can't move. Run!" bit out Katrina.

Desire to help her friends warred with self-preservation. Baby Viktor tipped the scale. She'd do anything to keep him safe. The blood dropped from Julie's hand, drawing the demon's attention.

Julie ran for the back door, yanked it open, and fled

into the night. Horror spurred her over the patio. When she hit the grass, Nicholai's strong voice sounded in her mind.

*What's wrong?*

*Nicholai, I need you. Now!* She sent him an image of what happened.

*I'm on my way. KEEP RUNNING!*

The night grew bright as day, and Julie glanced over her shoulder at the blonde demon.

Blue light surrounded the woman. Sparks flew in long streams from her nails. Her hair stood on end, flowing away from her scalp at least three feet.

Natasha appeared next to Julie and fell in step with her run. "Nicholai's coming."

"Take Viktor and run that way. She can't get us both at the same time."

At least, Julie hoped that was the case.

Natasha took the babe from her arms. Julie knew a moment of relief when the new mother hurled herself in the opposite direction. The respite passed quickly.

White hot light bathed over Julie, making her hair stand at attention. A strange calm overtook her, for Julie realized what was about to happen would give Natasha a chance to get to safety.

*Nicholai—*

*I'm dematerializing now, beloved.*

*I love—*

Blinding light bathed her in searing pain, then the world disappeared.

## Chapter 13

Nicholai materialized on the back lawn of Marcus' estate just as the bolt struck Juliette.

Their mindlink evaporated with a painful snap. *She can't be gone.*

*She isn't gone!*

A pile of dust settled on the grass for a second before the wind whipped it away.

"Nooooooooo!" Nicholai's voice faded as he dematerialized.

He kept his molecules a faint mist and floated to where she'd been. Her lilac scent surrounded him, mixed with the undeniable stench of burnt flesh and hair. Trying desperately to find a cell, an atom of his love, he breezed through the air. Swerved first one way then another. Back and forth in a pattern branching out from where he'd last seen her.

His soul ripped in two. Pain tore through him. Every cell cried for her at once. Frantically he reached for her, pushed his senses out, seeking the tiniest sign.

Nothing!

Dark, black, nothingness!

Juliette was gone.

Anger coursed through his blood, gave him purpose. He turned and headed for the demon bitch.

She gathered power to her and raised a hand above her head. White hot light coalesced in her palm. She shifted position and aimed the deadly energy at Natasha.

The heat burned his molecules, but he cared not. Revenge spurred him forward.

He took shape behind the demon. Blisters appeared on his flesh, pain burned every cell. Revenge his only thought, Nicholai thrust his hand through Jara's back and grabbed her heart. Her head turned on its shoulders. Evil and hatred flared in the fiery depths of her blood-red eyes. She opened her mouth, but only managed to let out a gasping scream before he snatched the foul thing out through the hole his hand created.

The electricity died with the bitch, taking the burn from his skin when her body collapsed. Nicholai threw the black heart on the ground and flattened it with the heal of his boot.

When the night grew dark once more, Natasha stopped running and turned to face him.

"Nicholai…Julie…" His sister didn't need to finish the sentence.

Grief fell on his shoulders. When the weight drove him to his knees, the cold, wet ground dug into his flesh. His arms crossed around his waist, and he bent forward until his forehead met the grass. Hot tears streamed from his eyes. Unbearable pain stabbed along every nerve.

His heartmate, the other half of his soul was gone. He'd never again hear her sweet voice, feel her soft skin. They would never walk in the moonlight or have the family they'd wanted so desperately.

*Nicholai, I'm here.* Demetri's voice sounded over their mindlink, but Nicholai blocked him. He didn't want to speak to anyone.

He crawled to the spot where Julie had been. Nicholai shoved his hands through the grass desperate to find a little warmth, anything that would prove she'd been there just moments before. But the ground provided no comfort.

His hands fisted in the blades, ripping them from the earth. Tears rolled down his cheeks. He sat back on folded legs and a sorrowful wail pushed from his lips. Anguish shook his body. Impossible to breathe, he welcomed the added pain of suffocation. Wished it would take him to his heartmate.

Natasha advanced. Determined not to let anything desecrate the spot, he lifted a staying hand. "Stop!"

"Nicholai, let me help you."

Through blurry tears, he watched as one by one the Alphas materialized behind Natasha and Viktor. They moved as a unit, encircling him. Christina joined them, followed by Katrina. They stood on either side of Tatiana. The women's cries joined with Nicholai's, filling the night.

Nicholai remained kneeling, his body shaking. Time lost all meaning. With Julie gone, nothing mattered. He buried his face in his hands, wishing he'd wake up from this nightmare.

Natasha laid a hand on his back. "Brother," tears choked her next words.

Instead of voicing her thoughts, she handed the baby to Vlad and knelt beside him. Her arms encircled his shoulders. Nicholai's hand clasped her arm, gripped it like a vice as if she'd be the next to go should he ever let go.

As they sobbed together, the group pulled in, each touching him. Hands lay on his back and head, arms folded around his chest. The ones who loved him most, held him in a collective hug. Just held him. They asked nothing, offered no words for they understood nothing said would take his pain. They simply held him, supported him while his grief brought the torment of a thousand suns.

Nicholai didn't know how long he'd been kneeling, didn't care. He didn't want to leave the last place Julie had been.

"Nicholai, the sun will rise soon." Natasha softly voiced the observation. "We must get inside."

He'd happily meet the fiery end sunup would bring if it meant he'd see Juliette once more. "I'm not leaving," Nicholai's voice broke on a sob.

## Chapter 14

When the pink hues of dawn painted the sky, the Alphas and their mates pulled away from Nicholai.

"Nicholai, you must go inside," Demetri whispered.

"Why? Without my Juliette, I have no reason to go on."

His sister rose to her feet. "Julie would not want you to do this, Nicholai."

Natasha's weak voice was almost his undoing. His stomach churned, and his dinner made a reappearance.

"She would want you to go on," Tasha continued, "even though it will be the most difficult thing you have ever done."

The loss of Juliette would always own a place in his heart, his soul. How was he supposed to go on when the one person who gave him comfort, the one person he wanted to be with wasn't there?

"Come," Demetri reached his meaty hands under Nicholai's arms to lift him to his feet and drew Nicholai beneath his shoulder. "We must get inside."

"You go," Nicholai offered, refusing to move.

"I'll not go without you," Demetri announced.

"Nor will I." Vlad stepped in front of Nicholai and handed Viktor to Natasha. "Take the baby into the house, Tasha. He doesn't need to see his father and uncles burn to death."

Nicholai's gaze roamed the faces of his brethren, his friends.

One by one the other Alphas announced they too would remain while they instructed their mates to go inside. The burden of causing their mates to endure the pain he must slowly forced reason into his mind. He would not be responsible for bringing that kind of grief to others.

One foot moved toward the home. Every cell screamed in protest. He hated leaving where she'd been. The other foot stepped. The torment increased. One slow stride at a time, he and the Alphas headed for the plantation house.

The sun's rays touched their skin. Smoke rose from their bodies, but not one of the warriors, not even Tatianna, said a thing. They simply formed a semi-circle behind Nicholai and let him set the pace to the home. Their silent resolve and support spurred him forward.

Once inside the home, Christina and Kat greeted them with bags of blood which the Alphas readily drank to aid their healing.

When Nicholai waved off the offer, Christina's tears flowed. "Nicholai, you need blood."

"I don't deserve any. Had I arrived sooner, I could have saved Juliette."

"Don't do that, Nicholai," Natasha rounded on him. "Don't. The fault of what happened tonight lies with that demon and her alone. You were fighting Eldrick. You left as soon as you could."

"Tasha." Vlad laid a smoldering hand on her shoulder. "Why don't you go put Viktor down? I'll make sure your brother gets to sleep."

Natasha rested a hand on Nicholai's arm. "Promise me we will talk tonight."

Nicholai nodded.

"Say it. Your word is your bond. Tell me you will speak with me when the sun sets."

Their eyes met, and Nicholai recognized the pain in her brown depths. His sister didn't think he'd make it through the day without sneaking out to meet the sun. He'd give her one day. As for the next one, well…

"I promise. We will speak after the sun sets."

Relief eased the lines around her bloodshot eyes. "Thank you."

She leaned over and kissed Vlad. "I'll see you in our chamber soon?"

He gave her a weak smile. "Soon."

Alex patted Nicholai's shoulder and shook his head without making eye contact. His hand trailed down Nicholai's bicep before the warrior headed up the stairs. Desmond moved in front of Nicholai.

"I loved her too." Tears pushed from Desmond's eyes when their gazes locked. "I…we…"

"I know," Nicholai choked out.

Desmond nodded and wiped the tears away, then dematerialized.

Stephan stood before Nicholai, sympathy glistening in his eyes. "You have a difficult day ahead. I want you to remember we are all here for you. Our greatest strength is when we fight as one. We now stand as one with you to get you through this, my brother."

Nicholai nodded, his words choked by emotions.

Katrina hugged him soundly, and her hot tears fell against his neck. "When I doubted Stephan, you were there for me. Now, I am here for you."

She kissed his cheek then Stephan drew her under the protection of his arm and led her up the stairs.

Marcus and Christina stepped forward.

Christina took Nicholai's hands in her ice-cold ones. "I want to tell you everything will be okay. I want to assure you each day the pain will lessen." She pursed her lips in a tight smile. "It won't. Not for a while. But I promise, one day you will find it easier to breathe. One day you will cry a little less. Those things I can promise, but you must fight through this time to find those days."

Marcus laid his hand over theirs. "Shit. I don't know what to say."

Nicholai's gaze met his. "There is nothing to be said. Nothing will make things easier this day."

Marcus shook his head then led Christina by the hand down the hall toward their bedroom, pulling her into a hug when sobs shook her body.

Tatiana moved in next. "She will stay with you for all time. Here." She placed a hand over his heart. "She will go where you go. Be where you are, as long as, you keep her with you in your heart."

After tapping his chest twice, she turned and headed upstairs.

Vlad and Demetri boxed him in on either side.

"Let's go to your room," his cousin suggested.

The trio mounted the stairs, each step a bigger burden than the last for Nicholai. When they arrived at his room, Demetri opened the door and the aroma of lilac flowed over him. Nicholai took the delicious scent deep into his lungs, committed it to memory, lest one day he forget it. His eyes closed of their own volition, forcing tears over his cheeks.

He needed to hold her. Needed to hear her sweet voice, just one more time. Needed the sound of her delicate laugh, the one that brightened his evenings.

But his nights would never again be bright.

Lost in grief, he barely took notice of Demetri and Vlad undressing him and placing him in the bed.

Both spoke before they left, but the words didn't register. When the door clicked shut behind them, Nicholai rolled over and clasped the pillow laying on the opposite side of the bed. Her pillow. It smelled like Julie. Each squeeze engulfed him in her scent.

He hugged the pillow over and over, burying his face in the linen, promising the Fates anything if they would only exchange his heartmate for the pillow. His woeful cries echoed in the empty room.

As he lay in the bed alone, the only thing touching him was the cool sheet which the night before had been warmed by Juliette. Thoughts of her consumed him. Memories of them ice skating and horseback riding skirted through his mind. Kept him from sleep.

He spent the day committing to memory the feel of her skin, the taste of her kiss. Determined not to have any memories fade, he replayed every special second they'd shared.

And when the sun set that day, for a moment, just the briefest of moments, he felt her. As if she'd come back to say goodbye, he sensed her delicate hand on his cheek. In that moment, Nicholai realized he'd do whatever it took to be with her again.

## Chapter 15

Alex strolled down the hall. The aftermath of the death had turned Marcus' home into a wasteland. Eerily quiet, the plantation, like the occupants, was in mourning. Halting in front of the door, Alex rose a fist. It stopped inches from the wood. Maybe he shouldn't knock. Maybe Nicholai would still be sleeping.

*Yeah, right.* More than likely his fellow Alpha spent most of the day awake. From what he understood about heartmates, he doubted the male would ever get a good day's sleep again.

Alex pushed his fingers through his hair in frustration. He said nothing to the man last night because he didn't know what to say. Truth be told, he still didn't know what to say, but he couldn't let another night go by without expressing his sympathy.

He gave a quick knock before he lost his nerve.

"Come." The voice within sounded like a turbo with a clogged intake, shaky and feeble.

Alex opened the door. A large canopy bed filled the room with its four ornately carved posts and sheer blue material. At the foot of the bed sat a delicate wooden bench, on it a tray of untouched food and blood. Cradling a nightgown, Nicholai lay in the middle of the bed. His head turned in Alex's direction.

Alex took a deep breath, hoping like Hell the Fates would give him the perfect thing to say. Instead, he said the only thing that came to mind.

"Hey, man."

Nicholai nodded his acknowledgement.

Alex's gaze landed on the stool sitting in front of a vanity. Though his body ached from the fight the night before, he grabbed the dainty thing and placed it next to the bed. Nicholai rolled over to face him. The nightgown slid along for the ride.

During the day, the warrior had been transformed and not in a good way. Like someone who had been in a year-long coma without food or water, he was an exhausted shell of his former self. Grief etched deep lines around his eyes and across his forehead. Red veins surrounded the Alpha's amber eyes. Crimson blotched his complexion. Most of the burns from the sun's first rays had scabbed but not healed completely. Some of the wounds still wept a yellow ooze.

"When was the last time you drank some blood?"

Nicholai shrugged. "I don't remember."

"Did you have any last night?"

Nicholai shook his head.

Alex tried to rise, despite his protesting muscles. "I'll pop down and get you some. Nothing like the right lube to keep a motor running."

Nicholai placed a stilling hand on Alex's arm. "I can't eat. My stomach won't keep anything down. It would be a waste."

"Nothing? What about some toast or applesauce? That's what my mama used to give me for an upset stomach."

A grimace took Nicholai's face. "When I think of food, I cramp. I've been vomiting all day."

"Shit." Alex sat. "I'm so sorry. I don't know what

to say. Julie was a great gal. She was fun and sweet. I'll miss her."

A tear escaped Nicholai's eye. "Me too."

Damn. He'd said the wrong thing. "Do you want to talk it out, man?"

"What I want is her back."

He couldn't give his friend that, but maybe he could give the warrior a second of thinking about something else.

"How about I fill you in on what you missed after you left the fight with Eldrick?"

Nicholai nodded, but his hands tightened around Julie's nightgown.

"So, before you left, we were kicking Eldrick's ass pretty good. We had the dude down, pummeling him. It looked like we might win. Then, all of a sudden, he sends out this burst of energy. I've never experienced anything like it. It threw us all off of him at once, sent us sailing about forty feet in the air. The second our asses hit the ground, he disappeared. No puff of smoke. No sulfur smell. Just disappeared. Have you ever seen anyone do that? Disappear and leave no trace behind?"

Nicholai shook his head.

When he didn't speak, Alex continued. "So, we all got up, shook off the pain, and were like 'what the fuck'. I mean, shit, we've never gone up against someone so powerful. He's unstoppable. The guy took all of us on and still got away."

"He is a most impressive opponent."

Tension eased from Alex's shoulders. Finally, the guy was talking. Maybe he'd chosen the right topic.

"I couldn't believe it when he picked up Demetri with one hand and tossed him so far into the air he needed to dematerialize to keep from hurting himself in the fall back down. Your cousin weights a ton, but don't go telling him I said that."

A slight smile raised a corner of Nicholai's mouth. "We can keep it between us."

Alex gave a snorting laugh. "Thanks. Last thing I need is Demetri or that female of his taking offense."

"She is rather defensive of him," Nicholai pointed out. The corner of his mouth dropped. "That is what heartmates do, defend each other. It is what I should have done."

Nicholai's grief flowed over Alex. His stomach knotted. "You did that."

"I did not. By the time I arrived, it was too late. When Juliette needed me, I was not there."

"Because you were fighting The Source. It's not like you were lying on a beach somewhere. You were helping us take out an enemy. We had all hands on deck and were still getting our asses kicked. When you left, any advantage we had left with you. Eldrick gave better than he got once the number was only seven to one."

"So not only did I let Juliette down but the Alphas as well."

Damn it! He'd meant to cheer Nicholai up, not make him feel worse. "That's not what I meant. I'm just pointing out you were in an impossible situation. You were needed in two places at once, and there is only one of you."

"He's right, you know." Natasha's voice startled Alex.

"I didn't hear you come in. How long have you been there?"

Tasha's weak smile didn't show her teeth. "Long

enough to know my brother is trying to blame himself for everything that went wrong last night."

"I am to blame." Nicholai rolled onto his back. Julie's nightgown draped across his torso.

As Natasha crossed the room, Alex rose from the stool. A sweep of his hand offered the seat to her, and she accepted with a nod.

"Brother mine, if you are to blame then so am I."

Nicholai's eyes locked with Natasha's. "How can you say that?"

"You sent me to Julie as soon as she called to you for help. I should have done something to save her."

Nicholai shook his head. "You saved Viktor."

Natasha laid a hand on her brother's. "Not to mention, it was Vlad and I who came across Eldrick last night and called the Alphas to the scene. Had we not been out on a date, we would not have come upon him, and there would not have been a fight."

Alex shifted his weight to his other foot and flinched when a shot of pain hit his brain from his not quite healed ankle. "But the demon attacked here while we were busy with Eldrick. That was not a coincidence. Attacking on two fronts suggests a planned attack."

Nicholai closed his eyes and took a heavy breath. "There was nothing you could do, Tasha. Eldrick and his minion are to blame."

Natasha patted Nicholai's hand. "Exactly, brother." She lowered her tone. "Exactly."

*Dang, she's good*, Alex thought.

"I think I'll bug on out of here. Stephan said he wanted to talk tonight, and no one keeps Stephan waitin' long." Alex placed a hand on Nicholai's shoulder. "Before I go, I have to tell ya, how sorry I am, man. There just aren't the right words."

Nicholai nodded. "Thank you."

Alex's hand dropped to his side, and he wished like Hell he knew some magic words which would take the pain from the warrior's eyes.

Alex limped across the room. "I'll see you both later."

"Bye," Natasha called out as he closed the door behind him.

He turned and ran into Stephan. "I was just coming to see you."

"I felt like this couldn't wait. Let's talk while we walk."

Alex decided not to comment on the way the warrior looked. Even after some blood and healing throughout the day, the male showed multiple signs of battle. Bruises darken his flesh. One eye appeared bloodshot. Like Alex, he sported multiple gashes where his flesh had yet to knit over the muscle and sinew.

The two moved side by side through the long hallway toward the stairs.

"So, what did you want to discuss?"

"Last night, when we left Eldrick and returned here to support Nicholai, I found Katrina and Christina in tears."

"Of course. I'm sure they saw what happened to Julie."

"No, that's not it. They were crying because they'd been trapped. Jara controlled their bodies somehow. She forced them to remain frozen and went after Juliette."

Surprise widened Alex's eyes. "She used mind control? I didn't know demons could do that."

Stephan shrugged. "I'm not sure what she did. That's why I need you to return immediately to the demon compound."

"But I planned on staying here for a few days. At least until the burial rite is performed."

"There won't be a ritual." A grim frown pulled the corners of Stephan's mouth down. "There's no body."

"Will there at least be a funeral of some kind?"

"I'm sure there will be, but not until Nicholai is feeling up to it."

"That will be a while," Alex commented as they started down the stairs.

"Exactly. In the meantime, I need you to go back to Wyoming and press Varrick into sharing all information about the demons and The Source. I get the impression the king hasn't told us everything he knows, and it's about time he coughs up the intel. Eldrick is unlike anything we've faced before, and we need help to defeat him."

"You can say that again. I see your wounds have not completely healed either."

Stephan glanced down at the arm through which a bone protruded the previous evening. His finger traced the pink wound of new skin over the sinew.

"Eldrick did not escape unscathed himself. We need to find him and attack again before he heals fully."

"So, you need the intel fast."

When they reached the bottom of the steps, Stephan stopped and turned toward Alex. "I need the intel tonight. I want to hit Eldrick again tonight or tomorrow at the latest. I need you, Alex. I need you to find out everything you can about The Source. We must know how to defeat him, and I'd be willing to bet everything I own that Varrick knows how to do that."

Determination straightened his spine. "I'll leave now."

The males grasped forearms in the way of the warrior. "Safe travels, Alex."

Alex nodded and dematerialized.

After his form coalesced inside the compound, his boots beat feet to the Throne Room. When the guards tried to stop him, he shoved them both away. "I don't have time to play today, fellas. I need to see the king."

He pushed through the heavy door, determined to get the information they needed. The sight of Shira on her knees stopped him.

"Please," she begged. "There must be something you can do. He can't die."

Varrick leaned forward. "What would you have me do?"

Alex moved closer. Concern drew his brows down over his eyes. "What's wrong?"

Shira's sob shook her body. The sight caused a pain in his chest, and he tried hard to rub the thing away.

Elizabeth rose from her chair and went to Shira to put a comforting arm around the demon.

"It's her nephew," the queen informed him. "He's ill."

"How? With what?"

"We don't know," Varrick pinned Alex with a stabbing glare. "But apparently the child acquired the illness from an excursion to the city."

*Shit!* Alex's last meal threatened to splash all over the rock floor.

"Cool Town," Alex supplied.

"It would seem so," Varrick replied coldly as his guards ran into the room. The king raised a stilling hand and leaned back in the throne. "Tell me bloodsucker, did you intend to kill all of us or was it a lucky happenstance."

Shock dropped Alex's mouth open, and the guards advanced to his sides. "What the Hell are you talkin' about? I didn't kill anyone."

"Not yet, but you will be responsible. You took the child to a place he could be infected. Now he brought an illness back to the compound. It is just a matter of time until it runs through all of us like a plague."

His stomach seemed to drop to his knees. Alex crossed his arms over his chest. "But that wasn't my intention. I simply wanted the little guy to have some fun."

Varrick rose. His red eyes glowed with anger. "If that is true, and I'm not sure I believe you, then your fun cost us our lives."

Alex raised his hands in surrender. "Whoa. I never meant to hurt anyone. I wouldn't do that. Shira, you believe me, right?"

The pretty demon turned her head and gazed up at him with tearful eyes. "I want to believe you, Alex. I thought you were a good guy. I even started to like you. To trust you. But now…I don't know what to think."

This was going belly up fast. He'd never intended to hurt anyone, especially the heart of the little demon kneeling on the floor. "You *can* trust me. I am a good guy, Shira."

Desperation pushed a thought into his head. "Take me to Tyler. I can save him."

"How?" asked Elizabeth while she helped Shira

stand.

"If I give him my blood, it will heal him."

Okay, so Stephan forbid anyone from exchanging with a demon, but this was different. We weren't talking an exchange between mates. This was life or death.

"Your blood can heal?" Shira sounded astonished. She glanced at Varrick with a hopeful expression. "Please, Varrick, allow him to try."

"What if he lies? What if it is a trick that will hasten the boy's death?"

Alex stepped forward, and the guards immediately grabbed his arms. He pulled against the restraint. Varrick rose. When he approached, the Alpha stopped struggling.

"How do you know what your blood will do to the child? Have you given blood to a demon before?" The king gave him an assessing glare.

"Look, Varrick, I haven't given a demon my blood, but I've given plenty of vampires and even a few humans my blood. Vampire blood has healing properties in it. It might cure Tyler."

"Varrick," Elizabeth moved to his side, "It can't hurt for him to try."

"Please." Shira's plea drew Varrick's attention. "Give him a chance to heal my nephew."

Varrick turned the power of his stare on Alex once more. "Very well. I'll let you share your blood with the boy. But know this, vampire, if it kills him, you will be the next to die."

Alex understood that was no threat. It was a promise, pure and simple. *Fuck! This better work.*

****

Shira and Elizabeth passed through the door with Varrick close behind. Alex got a personal escort from the two guards all the way to her room. As they walked, Shira reminded herself not to get her hopes up. This might not work. And what if it did? Would she owe Alex for saving Tyler's life? And just what might he ask from her in return?

When they entered the room, Alex pulled his arms free from the guards' steely grips. "I'll need these, if I'm to help."

Alex's strides took him to the bed where Tyler lay. The child shivered under the blankets. Sweat beaded on his forehead and arms. Alex placed a hand on the boy's forehead. The child moaned.

"What's he doing here?" Talia asked from where she sat on the bed.

Shira moved to her sister's side. "He said he can cure Tyler."

Talia's hopeful eyes met Alex's. "Is that true?"

"I think my blood will heal him."

Varrick cleared his throat. "You must be told, Talia, it is a supposition. The vampire's blood has healed others, but it's never been tried on a demon. We don't know what will happen."

"How does it work?" Talia asked.

"My blood contains healing properties. If he drinks a little of it, it should cure him."

Shira squeezed her sister's hand. "Let him try, Talia. It's Tyler's only hope. We lost his father to illness. We can't lose him too."

Talia nodded her head. "Very well, do it."

With no time to waste, Alex scored his wrist with his fangs and placed the wound over the child's lips.

"Drink, my sweet boy," his mother pleaded as she triggered his swallowing reflex by stroking his throat.

Tyler's tongue licked Alex's arm then the child took a long pull of his blood. Hope flooded Shira when Tyler swallowed. This had to work. *It must!*

After two more swallows, relief blossomed in Shira's chest. The perspiration disappeared from Tyler's brow. He ceased shivering. His eyes opened, and the vampire pulled his arm away.

"I think that's enough."

Tyler looked at his mother. "Hi, Mommy."

"Tyler," Talia cried out in joy. She pulled the boy into her arms and squeezed him tight. "You're okay. I was so scared."

"Why, Mommy?"

She rocked the child. "You got sick, but Alex made you better."

Tyler smiled at him from over his mother's shoulder. "That's 'cause he's a good guy. Right, Aunt Shira?"

She pulled her gaze from her nephew and locked eyes with Alex. Jubilation lightened Shira's heart. Tyler was better. She fell into the depths of Alex's light blue eyes. If she wasn't careful, she might have to admit she felt more than just gratitude.

She liked Alex. Maybe more than liked him if she was being honest with herself. Okay, fine, Shira reasoned. This had potential. He was incredibly sexy, and he had a fun sense of humor. Oh crap! She wanted to explore a relationship with the guy.

The expectant expression on Alex's face was endearing. Shira smiled a wide grin, hoping her joy and appreciation showed. "That's right, Tyler. Alex is a good guy."

Varrick drew Elizabeth under the protection of his arm. "I think we need to give the family a bit of privacy."

"I agree." Elizabeth put an arm around Varrick's waist. "Let's all go back to the Throne Room, so we can talk."

Elizabeth pinned Alex with a pointed stare, and he gave a nod of acknowledgment.

Elation pushed Shira off the bed. She wrapped her arms around the vampire's waist. "Thank you!"

Alex returned the embrace and pulled her against the muscular plains of his body. It felt good to be in his arms. Felt right.

"I'm glad it worked." His deep voice rumbled in his chest against her ear.

Before common sense stopped her, she rose on her tiptoes, grabbed his face between her hands and kissed him. Her tongue forced through his lips. Her taste mingled with his for a brief second before the king cleared his throat.

"We were going," Varrick pointed out.

Alex broke the kiss and glared at the demon then he glanced back at Shira. "I think that is my cue. I'll return after Varrick and I have a chat."

Shira smiled. "I'll be here."

She watched him leave with the royal entourage. When the door clicked shut behind them, images of him stalking through the hall with an ease of power and grace flooded her mind.

He was tall, handsome. When his vampiric instincts receded, he was just as polite and friendly as any demon. Since the first time she'd laid eyes on him, there had been a pull between them that strengthened over time. Goddess help her, even his scent no longer repulsed her. The odorous stench of vampire had become musky and darkly spiced. It made her crave him more. It was almost as if…as if…

Her hand reached for the bed to steady herself.

*We can't be mates. It isn't possible!*

"What's wrong," Talia asked around Tyler.

Shira shook her head. "Nothing. Just a little dizzy from all the excitement."

*And from possibly being mates with a vampire*, her inner voice supplied.

Her heart leapt for joy in her chest.

Oh, Goddess help her! She was attracted to Alex. No, wait. Change that. She had the hots for him something fierce. Who wouldn't want to kiss every inch of that hard body with those hips, hollow and jutting out from under the skin, and thick arms that felt amazing around her? Sure, he had a ribbed abdomen and pretty-boy looks. And sure, he had all that flirty sexiness going for him. And, yeah, maybe her libido wanted to take him out for a test drive, but they were opposite ends of the spectrum. Two different breeds. It was impossible for them to be mates.

Wasn't it? Her heart did another flipflop behind her ribs.

****

Alex followed Varrick and Elizabeth down the corridor with the guards hot on his heels. When they arrived in the Throne Room, the couple stepped on the dais and sat in their chairs. Really it was a bit too pomp and circumstancy for Alex's tastes, but he guessed the king needed to keep up appearances.

Alex stopped by the platform and clasped his hands in front of him. Varrick eyed him up and down. His eyes held knowledge, and Alex recognized the perfect opportunity to do what he'd come here to do.

"You proved yourself today, vampire," said Varrick.

"I'm glad you trusted me enough to let me try."

Varrick placed a thoughtful hand on his chin. "I suppose you earned it."

"I'd like to have more of your trust."

He stroked the blond stubble on his jaw. "What do you mean?"

"We fought The Source last night."

Varrick's eyes widened, and his hand fell to the armrest. "Did you defeat him?"

"No, but…" Should he share what happened to Jara? She was the king's sister after all. Maybe now wasn't the time, not since he needed to keep the king's trust and cooperation.

"But what," Varrick prompted.

"But he is too powerful. Have you found anything to help us defeat him?"

Elizabeth nodded her head, sending her golden locks swaying. "Tell him, Varrick."

"Shhhh, Little Bits."

Alex didn't have time for this covert bullshit. "Look. We put a hurtin' on Eldrick last night. Stephan wants to attack again before he has a chance to heal completely."

"So that is the reason for your injuries?"

"What?" Alex glanced down at his hands and arms. "Yeah. We jumped Eldrick, but we need help. He's too strong to defeat hand to hand. If you know something that can help, we need to know what it is."

"There might be something I can share, but I'll only give it directly to Stephan."

"Great! Let's go. You can call him."

"I want to see him in person."

Shira burst into the room, appearing disheveled.

"Is everything all right?" asked Elizabeth.

"It's Tyler," Shira puffed out on a breathy voice.

Fear and concern gripped Alex's heart. Did his blood only provide the child a partial recovery? Had Tyler relapsed?

Shira clasped her hands together. "I couldn't wait to tell you. It's a miracle. Tyler is not only fine. He's better than fine. He can do things now he couldn't do before."

Varrick leaned forward. "Such as?"

Shira glanced at Alex when she passed him to approach the dais. "He has super strength. He picked the entire bed up from the floor and crushed a toy between two fingers. He also can dematerialize without leaving a trace. Most amazing of all, he can levitate!"

"He can *what*?" Varrick and Alex asked simultaneously.

"Levitate!" Excitement made Shira's voice louder. "I swear he floated so high, Talia couldn't reach him."

"I'll be damned." Alex placed a hand over his mouth.

"It has to be the vampire blood," Shira informed them. "Nothing else can explain it."

"If my blood did that to Tyler, I wonder what would happen if a vampire drank demon blood." All eyes fell on Alex. He shrugged. "Just wondering."

Elizabeth leaned forward and squinted her eyes on

him. "Let's find out."

"Elizabeth!" Varrick admonished. "What are you thinking?"

She turned her demure face to the king and grabbed his hand. "I'm thinking we might have just found the way to defeat The Source. What if by sharing blood, both demons and vampires become more powerful?"

Varrick's brows furrowed over his red eyes before he turned them on Alex. "What do you think?"

"I think we could test it out. I could drink your blood."

"I think not! You will not be tasting my blood tonight." His gaze shifted to Shira. "However, there is another alternative."

Shira put her hands up in surrender. "Now hold on a second, I didn't agree to anything."

"As your king, I don't require your agreement."

"However," Elizabeth interrupted. "It would be helpful if you'd willingly donate."

Alex's nerves frazzled. Was he ready to experiment like this?

He shifted onto his hurt foot pleasantly surprised to find it healed. "What if something goes wrong? What if I die?"

"That's a chance I'm willing to take," Varrick informed him with a smile.

"What do you say, Shira?" Elizabeth asked. "Will you give a little blood to Alex, so we can see what happens?"

"I guess so." Shira faced Alex and held out her wrist. "Go ahead."

Stephan's directive warred in Alex's mind. He'd explicitly said not to exchange blood with demons. It was bad enough he'd given his blood to one, but there had been extenuating circumstances. This would be a blatant disregard of the order. On the other hand, if her blood gave him new powers then exchanging blood with the demons might just be the way to defeat Eldrick.

His gaze moved from Shira's wrist up her arm to her neck. If that sexy demon was offering, he sure as Hell had no intention of taking from her wrist. Their eyes met, and he smiled.

"I'd gladly accept your offer." He moved closer and took her wrist in his hand. As he lowered her arm he continued, "But your wrist is not where I'll draw from."

Alex snaked an arm around her waist and drew her close. He buried his face in the delicate spot where her shoulder met her neck and took a deep inhale of her rosy scent. His fangs lengthened in anticipation.

Alex's tongue darted out to taste her flesh. Goosepimples appeared as she shivered in his arms. His fangs scraped against the bumps before they sank into her skin. A contented moan pushed through her red lips.

Blood coated his throat. The first swallow warmed his body. Each cell cried for more. The world tilted on its axis.

*MINE!* The thought exploded in his mind. His inner beast roared to life. It craved her. Wanted her. The shock of needing her with a desire never before experienced broke his concentration.

He jerked his head from her neck and stared down on her. "You're my—"

Her hand flew to the wounds on her neck. "Your what?"

Alex gently pulled her fingers from the fang marks and licked them closed. Now was not the time to find a heartmate, especially a demonic one. They had a battle looming, and no one knew who would walk away the winner. There couldn't be a worse time to announce they were mates. After they won, he'd confess.

Luckily, Varrick kept him from needing to answer her question. "Well, vampire, how do you feel?"

*Surprised. Elated. Horny. Pick one or better yet, how about all of the above?*

Alex licked his lips and smiled. "I feel great."

His motor was growling like a well-tuned Hemi.

"I meant do you feel any different?" Varrick leaned forward.

Alex did a quick assessment. "I feel better."

Finding his mate was like driving a high-end race car, energizing and thrilling. His blood was pumping on all cylinders.

"Your wounds are healed," Elizabeth observed.

Alex glanced at his arms then rolled his hands, examining the backs and palms. Sure enough, no sign of last night's fight remained. He put on a burst of speed and raced around the room in record time, coming to a stop back beside Shira. "I'm faster."

"Can you levitate?" asked Shira.

Alex shrugged. "Let's see."

He lifted Shira into his arms and envisioned his body rising to the ceiling. They rose effortlessly. He gazed into her red eyes lovingly. "I'd say I can levitate."

Shira smacked his arm. "Put me down."

Alex pretended to drop her. She squealed and threw her arms around his neck. "Safely! Put me down, safely!"

Alex chuckled and floated them down. "I'd never hurt you, darlin'."

It felt good to have her in his arms. Felt right, like coming home. He reluctantly placed her feet on the floor. Her body slid sinuously down his, making his libido stand at attention.

"I believe we have discovered how to defeat The Source," Varrick announced.

"We need to tell Stephan," Alex said. "I think Shira should come along too, just to confirm the story."

Of course, the real reason he wanted her by his side was he had no intention of letting his heartmate out of his sight so soon after finding her.

To the warrior's surprise, Varrick nodded. "I agree. I have a suspicion Stephan will need some convincing."

*You have no idea.* Not only did he worry about convincing Stephan but to do so would require him to confess he'd gone against orders.

Alex scrubbed a hand down his face, pulling the skin taut. *Stephan's gonna kill me.*

## Chapter 16

"I could kill you!" Stephan's roar brought people to the living room.

*Well, this is going as expected*, thought Alex.

Varrick crossed his arms over his massive chest as the remainder of the occupants in the plantation house joined the Alphas.

Katrina stepped next to her mate. "What in the world is going on?"

"Alex here was filling me in on the intel he's gathered from the demons."

Varrick's eyes narrowed before he stood. "Intel? I *knew* he was a spy."

Shira rose from her seated position between Varrick and Alex on the couch. "Varrick, it's not like I allowed him access to any secrets."

Stephan moved in front of Katrina. "I knew you were keeping secrets from us. We should never have trusted you. Harleigh was spying on us, wasn't she?"

The air around Harleigh turned blue from her aura. Desmond's arm snaked about her stomach and pulled her behind him. He positioned himself between the Alpha leader and the petite demon.

"She's no spy," Desmond assured.

"How do you know she hasn't been playing you? Playing all of us?" Tatiana crossed her leather-clad legs.

Alex had had enough. The warrior stood and raised his arms. "The time for distrust is over. We have a problem much bigger than who saw what."

Alex faced the demon king. "The time for secrets has passed. You must share everything you know about The Source."

"And you," Alex turned to Stephan, "must share everything as well. The two of you have been so worried about the other finding out your abilities you haven't told one another what you need to know."

Harleigh moved in front of Desmond. "He's right. Varrick, these people are honorable and trustworthy. In my time with them, they have consistently demonstrated fairness. Sure, there were times when tempers flared, but they never treated me poorly."

Desmond wrapped his arms around the blue-haired demon. "And some of us treated her like a queen."

Harleigh's arms laid over Desmond's, and she settled back against him.

Varrick's hands fisted by his side. "You mean you and this vampire are together?"

Alex tucked Shira under his arm. "So, what if they are? There is nothing wrong with a vampire and demon falling in love."

"Love?" Shira's light brows shot up on her forehead.

Vlad scraped a hand over his black goatee. "I think we got off subject. We should be swapping information."

"Agreed." Varrick sat back down on the couch. "Share."

"You first," Stephan prompted.

Alex rolled his eyes. He pulled Shira down on the

couch. As they sat, her leg brushed his, sending an electrical current through him. His hand found her long hair, so his fingers could brush through the silky strands as he spoke.

"I'm tired of this nonsense. No disrespect to the leaders in the room, but you two are about as stubborn as a two-headed mule tryin' to decide which way to go. We need to stop the posturing, and our breeds start working together."

"I agree." Desmond pulled Harleigh down with him on the opposite couch.

"That's because you are thinking with your dick," Demetri commented in a low voice.

Desmond shifted toward the Russian Alpha. "Actually, I'm thinking with my head, old man. We can do more together than separate. The demons have some pretty impressive powers."

Alex nodded. "Yeah, like this." He lifted his hands and tiny sparks shot from his fingers.

"You can create energy?" Varrick appeared astonished.

Alex grinned. "I can now since I drank Shira's blood."

"Can you throw a flame?"

Alex shrugged one shoulder. "Don't know."

"Try," Shira encouraged him. "Try to start a fire in the fireplace."

Alex focused on his right hand, trying to force the energy to coalesce into a ball of fire as he'd witnessed other demons do. White light glowed. Heat warmed the hand. He tossed it toward the hearth. It fell short and landed on the carpet inches from Katrina's shoes.

Stephan jumped into action and stamped out the

flame.

Varrick chuckled. "Not very impressive."

"Maybe I need a reboot," Alex suggested. "Maybe the effects of the blood are temporary."

"Why don't you find out?" Shira pulled her platinum locks over one shoulder, exposing her neck. "Take another sip."

When he hesitated, she added, "I actually liked it."

He'd be damned if he'd let the opportunity to sip his mate's blood pass. His fangs lengthened from his gums. Anticipation of the fiery taste on his tongue made him salivate. Her blood was unlike any he'd had before, and he'd never get enough. "Well, if you're sure you don't mind."

He leaned in and breathed her delicious rosy scent into his lungs. His fangs slid into her creamy flesh, and sweet ambrosia flowed over his taste buds. Every cell exploded with power. Tingles covered his body. He drank his fill, ceasing only when Stephan yelled stop.

Alex licked the tiny wounds clean, leaned back and closed his eyes. His senses sharpened. Power coursed through his veins. He wrapped himself in it. When a collective gasp filled the room, the warrior opened his eyes and discovered a blue aura surrounded him.

"Try throwing fire now," Shira encouraged in a breathy voice.

Alex again focused on his right hand. A ball of white light formed instantly. He lobbed the volleyball-size globe into the fireplace. It exploded. Tender and bricks flew into the room set ablaze.

Everyone scrambled to put out the flames before they caused a fire.

"Sorry 'bout that," Alex offered. "I guess I don't

know my own strength."

"It would seem your strength is directly proportional to when you consume the blood," Stephan surmised.

Varrick nodded his head. "If that's the case, then your blood's effects should be temporary too. Shira, go to the compound, and see if your nephew can still levitate or has any of the other effects remaining."

"Did you say levitate?" Natasha asked, bouncing Viktor on her lap.

Shira and Alex rose in unison. "Let me see her off, and then I'll show you."

Alex escorted his mate to the foyer. Once out of sight from the others, he pulled her into his arms. "Don't be too long. I'll miss you."

Shira smiled and placed her hands on his chest. "Don't worry. It shouldn't take me long to pop over to the compound and find out if Tyler can still fly. If he can't, I'm sure I'll find him pouting about it when I arrive."

Alex chuckled and gave her a long kiss. Before he could wish her safe travels, she dematerialized from his arms leaving a sulfuric odor behind. His woman was something else. *Yeah, like a demon.* And didn't that just beat all?

As he returned to the living room, he shook his head at the irony. Stephan and Varrick pulled him from his rumination.

Stephan put his fisted hands on his hips. "There must be something you can tell us about The Source."

"We haven't found much."

The Alpha leader shifted his weight. "He's damned near impossible to kill. I've never fought a being so powerful. He can control multiple beings with his mind and dematerialize without a trace, no smell, no wisp of smoke."

"His strength is unsurpassed," Vlad added.

Tatiana nodded. "Not to mention he can heal faster than any of us."

Demetri placed a hand on the nape of Tatiana's neck. "Varrick, if you know anything, tell us."

"Even the smallest detail might help." All eyes turned to the quiet voice that spoke the sentence.

Nicholai entered the room looking like he'd been ridden hard and put away wet. The emaciated figure crossed the room on silent feet. His sister rushed to his side and hugged him sideways to avoid squishing the baby.

"Come, sit." Natasha led him to the couch across from Varrick.

Nicholai complied then stared at the demon. "You must share. We all must share."

"Nicholai, you need to drink and eat something," Katrina begged. "Please let me get you some blood at least."

The Russian warrior shook off thc offer with a wave of his hand. "Not now."

Varrick crossed his thick legs, resting an ankle on the opposite knee. "There is a tome I found which mentioned The Source. It claims he is the first of our kind."

"The first demon?" asked Vlad.

"The first of all our kinds." A confused murmur floated around the room. "According to the text, The Source is the first human to survive the plague. From him, vampires and demons evolved, each taking certain attributes."

"Son-of-a-bitch," Alex cursed.

"Could that be why Alex received demon powers when he drank Shira's blood?"

Varrick's hand grabbed his shin. "I believe when a vampire and demon exchange blood, each absorbs the other's powers."

"So, by exchanging blood, we might all become as powerful as Eldrick," Stephan hypothesized.

Varrick nodded. "Possibly. And there's more."

"Of course, there is." Tatiana rolled her cat-like yellow eyes, earning a look of admonishment from Stephan.

"Please continue," their leader encouraged the king.

"Elizabeth found a prophecy about The Source. It read, 'to kill the beast, still his beating heart and all will come to a fiery end.'"

"What the Hell does that mean?" Marcus pushed a hand through his brown hair.

Vlad cleared his throat. "Maybe it means if we pierce his heart, he'll burst into flame."

"That could be one possible interpretation," Varrick agreed.

Demetri crossed his large arms over his chest. "Another could be fire will kill Eldrick."

Varrick nodded. "True."

"So basically, the prophecy is no help." Christina pulled her red hair back from her face. "We still don't know how to kill Eldrick."

Stephan straightened. "However, maybe we don't need the prophecy. If we exchange blood with the demons, we'll possess the same powers as Eldrick.

Facing eight of us with the exact same powers would seem impossible odds."

Varrick cleared his throat. "I believe you meant to say *nine* of us. If I'm going to share my blood with you, then you will reciprocate and share your blood with me, so I can also fight."

The leaders locked eyes. After a moment of hesitation, Stephan said, "Of course. You are a warrior. We'd be honored to fight by your side."

Varrick inclined his head. "The honor will be mine. I think today is the start of a great alliance."

"Agreed."

Alex rubbed his palms along his jeans. "So now that we have that settled. What's the battle plan?"

"First, we must locate Eldrick."

Harleigh jumped up. "I can do that. I'll scry for him."

Tatiana eyed her wearily. "What's scrying?".

"Basically, I use a bowl of water and a rock to locate him."

"Sounds ridiculous."

Harleigh huffed.

"Is that how Jara found the plantation?" asked Nicholai.

"Probably." Varrick uncrossed his legs. "Speaking of my sister, where is she?"

"Dead, like my Juliette," spit out Nicholai. "I killed her."

Alex's gaze flew back to Varrick. Holy Hell, this might undo everything.

The king's eyes narrowed on the grieving warrior. "What did you say?"

Harleigh moved next to Varrick and took his hand

in hers. “I know Jara was your sister. She was my cousin. I used to love her like I do you. But holy crap on a cracker, she’d gone bad, Varrick. She attacked the women here and the baby.”

Varrick’s demeanor softened. “I’d hoped she could be saved.”

“Me too. But attacking women and a baby! Varrick, she needed to be stopped.”

“I know.” The king hung his head. “I just can’t believe my sister would do such a thing. What happened to the sweet little girl who played with me in the forest?”

Harleigh patted the king’s hand. “Hang onto those memories. I know I will.”

Varrick pursed his lips. “No time to grieve. We have a battle to prepare for.”

“Good onya. That’s the attitude I expect from my king.” Harleigh smiled. “Now, I’ll go scry for Eldrick. I’ll let you know when I find the bugger.”

As Harleigh left the living room, the Alphas and Varrick discussed strategy. Deciding strength in numbers would be their greatest asset, they agreed to overwhelm Eldrick by all attacking at once. By the time Harleigh returned with the location of The Source, they had exchanged blood and were juiced for a fight.

Shira popped into the middle of the room. “I’m back.”

“Report,” snapped Varrick.

Irritation at the king’s tone prickled up Alex’s spine. No one talked to his mate like that, even if no one yet knew they were mates. Before he could intervene, Shira spoke.

“Tyler returned to normal. The effects of the blood

have worn off."

Concern made Alex's stomach knot. "Does that mean the little guy is sick again?"

Shira shook her head. "He's fine. Your blood cured him."

A wide grin lit her face, and his world brightened. The happiness didn't last long.

"Eldrick's in the cemetery," Harleigh informed them.

"Which one?" asked Marcus. "There are several."

Harleigh faced Marcus. "One by a river."

"That's just outside of town."

"He's holed up in one of the mausoleums."

Stephan nodded. "We'll need to draw him out then."

"I'm sure we can find a way." A sly grin took Varrick's face.

Stephan nodded. "Everyone grab a weapon and get in the SUVs."

The warriors pilfered weapons from Marcus' cache. Alex glanced around the room, noting his fellow Alphas arming themselves. They were all adorned in clothing similar to what he wore, a black turtleneck tucked into black cargo pants, and heavy dark combat boots. Those with longer hair, like Stephan and Demetri, tied it back in a thong.

They each chose weapons to carry into battle. Vladimir preferred nine millimeters while Tatiana grabbed a pair of Sais. The light played off the long blades when she twirled them in her hands. Demetri palmed a titanium-coated sword and slung it over his back after tucking a forty-five into the waistband of his pants.

Alex chambered a titanium round in his semi-auto, then doubted he'd need the thing. With Varrick and Shira's blood in his veins, he felt invincible. There was a beast in every man that surfaced when he palmed a weapon, and luckily for him, demon blood fueled his beast tonight.

Marcus slung the crossbow over his shoulder and turned, eyes locking with Stephan's who palmed a few throwing stars and a dagger.

Alex noticed Nicholai didn't grab anything. "What you gonna take with you, man?"

Nicholai shrugged wearily. "Nothing appeals to me."

"Fightin' bare-knuckled, huh? That's badass." Alex flashed the warrior a sad smile.

Varrick snatched a sword and tested its sharpness gingerly with the pad of his thumb. "This will do."

"Load up," Stephan ordered.

The group scattered. Some headed for the vehicles, others for their mates. Alex found Shira in the kitchen.

"I'm leaving," he informed her.

She turned and hugged him around the waist. "Be safe."

"Worried about me?"

Her red eyes, with those fiery golden flecks, stared up at him. "Just come back here in one piece, you silly bloodsucker."

Maybe winning her love wouldn't be as difficult as he'd imagined. When he returned, he'd tell her she was his heartmate. In the meantime, there was no way he was going into battle without a proper send-off kiss.

He bent his head to hers and took her luscious lips in a thorough kiss. His tongue explored the recesses of her mouth. She tasted of chocolate and woman.

Her body melted against his. His arms wound around her back. Passion danced between them like an electric current. Sparks, literal sparks, flew from his fingers.

Shira pushed away. She held her hand over her mouth, hard breaths bursting through her fingers. "You almost caught my hair on fire."

"Sorry. I guess it will take a while to get used to these powers."

Shira nodded. "You better go."

Yeah, he better. And didn't that just suck. He hated leaving her, but duty called, and he always answered with a resounding *Hell, yes*.

"When I get back, we are going to have a talk."

"Count on it. We have a lot to discuss."

As Alex headed for the front door, he wondered what Shira meant.

## Chapter 17

Alex climbed from the SUV and scoped out the area. Spanish moss hung thickly from the oak trees looking like ethereal arms with long spindly fingers that reached for them. The heavy air smelled of rain and freshly cut grass. Doom settled over the warrior.

The graveyard laid beyond the iron gates. Somewhere within, Eldrick waited.

Demetri pulled Tatiana into his arms. "Listen, *kotik kisa*, if something should happen to me," he began, his tone serious. "If I fall, you must—"

"No." She shook her head in denial. "You won't fall."

"But if I do, don't do anything stupid. Don't come after me. Don't let me distract you."

"Demetri, I love you."

"I love you too, Tatiana. And I know you. You must promise me if I die, you'll not follow me into the Great Beyond."

Tatiana shook her head. "Don't ask me to do that."

Demetri grabbed Tatiana's shoulders. "Promise me. I can't go in there unless I know you'll be safe no matter what happens to me."

She shook her head again. "You promise me, you'll make it through this alive."

Suddenly the ground shook. An explosion sent detritus flying through the air to cover them. Alex spit out the dirt and looked up. The moon outlined a figure.

Eldrick floated down, landing in the middle of the group.

*So much for a sneak attack.*

Eldrick held his arms from his sides. "I see you've come to play, again."

Alex gave him a once over. He seemed no worse for wear. No injuries from the previous night remained. Too bad the Alphas couldn't boast the same.

"Give up now, Eldrick, and we'll let you live," Stephan offered as he moved around The Source.

Eldrick spun in a circle, tracking the Alpha leader. "I see you brought more backup this time. Too bad, it won't help."

Varrick moved in the opposite direction of Stephan, sword in hand. "Don't discount me." The king sent a streak of fire down the weapon. "I have a few tricks up my sleeve."

Eldrick laughed. "Perhaps you do. I could use some entertainment." He settled into a fighting stance. "Let's see what you can do."

As planned, Alex and the others remained back and gathered energy into the palms of their hands, while Stephan and Varrick advanced on Eldrick. With a swooshing sound, Varrick brought the broadsword down in a blazing arc. Eldrick caught the thing between the fingers of both hands. It stopped inches from his face and illuminated his skin with a red glow. An evil grin spread when Varrick shook with effort to finish the blow. Eldrick blew on the weapon, extinguishing the flame, then pulled it from Varrick's grasp and flung the thing in Stephan's direction, smoke trailing through the air. Their leader barely moved in time to avoid being bludgeoned. Unfortunately, the same could not be said of the Alpha behind him.

With a sickening slicing sound, the weapon slid through Marcus' gut and headed for the tree behind. The Alpha's energy ball fell to the ground. He grabbed his stomach to keep his guts from spilling out. Marcus moaned and dropped to his knees. Desmond's ball dissipated as he ran to help. The slice wasn't a killing blow, but it would put Marcus out of the fight while it healed.

As the sword embedded into the tree, Stephan yelled, "Now!"

The Alphas threw their energy balls at Eldrick. The Source's eyes widened slightly then he leapt into the air. The balls exploded in a fiery crash that created a blinding white light. As Alex's vision came back online, he witnessed Eldrick float back to the ground, some singed clothing the only evidence of their attack.

Eldrick grabbed Varrick and lifted him above his head. The demon shifted into a lion, giving the Alpha leader the opening he needed. Stephan launched a series of throwing stars. They hit Eldrick in the back, and his grip loosened. The demon king let out a mighty roar as he twisted and bit into Eldrick's shoulder. A raw scream of pain ripped from the Source before he threw Varrick to the ground with such force, the dirt swallowed the lion whole.

Stephan palmed a dagger and jumped on Eldrick's back. When Stephan brought the knife around his body, aiming for the throat, Eldrick's hand blocked the shot. The blade embedded in his palm. The Alpha leader drove the knife into Eldrick's flesh, but his hand not only stopped it from going too deep, it deflected the aim.

The Source used the injured hand to push the weapon from his shoulder. Stephan let go of the knife and grabbed Eldrick's head. Before he could give it a twist, Eldrick reached over his shoulders, grabbed Stephan in a steely grip, and pulled the warrior from his back. When the Alpha leader hit the ground, Eldrick gave him a kick to the head that snapped his neck.

Before Eldrick could administer a killing blow, Alex pulled his semi-auto from its holster and squeezed the trigger. The first round buzzed by Eldrick's ear. The second hit its mark. The force of the bullet spun The Source, and he rounded on Alex. As he got off a third round, an invisible force pulled the gun from his hand. Round three hit Eldrick in the chest just as the gun flew apart into a million pieces.

While Alex did a whole lotta what-the-fuck, Tatianna reached his side and muttered, "Eldrick must have done that with his mind."

With no time to think on that, they launched a simultaneous attack on Eldrick. Alex landed the first punch. A satisfying crunch filled the air. Tatiana did a swipe with her leg that brought Eldrick to the ground. Alex landed on his chest and reared back for the next blow. His hand punched the cold ground.

"What the Hell?"

Alex looked about. Eldrick materialized near Tatiana who stood in a fighting stance with a Sais in each hand. He grabbed her head between his palms. She stabbed the blades into his legs. When the pain didn't deter his attack, she released the weapons. Her hands grabbed his, but it was too late. He snapped her neck. She went down. Demetri roared and advanced with his forty-five blazing.

Round after round pierced Eldrick's flesh. He staggered as the beefy Alpha moved closer. Alex jumped to his feet and ran for the melee. With Eldrick's attention on Demetri, Alex dove for The Source, catching him around the waist. The motion sent the pair into Demetri. The three tumbled on the ground in a sea of limbs. An elbow rammed Alex's cheek. It swelled instantly from the blow. Something crunched into his knee, sending a fresh round of throbbing to his brain.

When they came to rest, Demetri laid on top of Alex, and Eldrick had disappeared. Alex rolled out from underneath Demetri in time to witness Varrick rise from the dirt once again in human form just as Vlad and Nicholai performed a coordinated attack.

Focused on Vlad and Nicholai, Eldrick didn't block Varrick. The king punched the back of Eldrick's head with lightning speed, over and over. The Source's head pulled a punching bag maneuver, snapping back and forth. Nicholai timed punches to his face perfectly with the bobbing of the head.

*We might just win this one,* thought Alex.

Then the unthinkable happened.

Vlad's gun flew apart just as Alex's had. Eldrick reached behind him, grabbed Varrick's leg, and pulled the king up so he dangled from Eldrick's grasp. The Source slammed the demon down on the ground, forcing him to do a split while Eldrick retained hold of the leg. He jerked the front leg up until it touched Varrick's face. Varrick howled and slumped on the ground. Eldrick let go to turn his attention on Nicholai.

The Source hit Nicholai in the chest with blurring speed until the warrior fell. Eldrick pounded Nicholai's breastplate over and over. It caved inward, and the Alpha went still.

Alex jumped back into the fight. He landed between Vlad and Demetri. The trio advanced, but Alex arrived first. He punched Eldrick's stomach. The Source bowed from the force of the blow, wrapped a firm hand around Alex's arm, and removed it from his stomach. He wrenched the arm behind Alex's back, dislocating it, and forced him to bend at the waist. The hurt was nothing compared to what was sure to come. Alex knew a moment of dread.

Eldrick's knee met his face in a series of quick blows. Bones crunched. Pain exploded in his head. His cheek broke, then his jaw. Alex's nose was mincemeat. His forehead caved inward. Blood filled his mouth, but the next blow forced it out before he breathed in too much of it. It spattered on the grass.

Eldrick used the dislocated arm to twist Alex's body for the next move. The Source grabbed his mangled face and wrenched. Alex's body flew through the air and landed hard against a tree. Leaves floated down from the branches while he struggled to remain conscious. Every breath shot agony through his entire body. A moan escaped his bloodied lips. Alex watched Eldrick advance through swollen eyes, knowing death would come to take the pain. The warrior welcomed the respite.

Stephan, having recovered from his broken neck, sent electricity from his fingers. The air around them crackled, a thunderous zap echoed in the night when the current found its mark. Eldrick's body jerked. Vlad and Demetri joined in to save Alex. Blue electricity streamed from the warriors' fingertips. Eldrick had no choice but to fire back.

Light exploded when the forces met. Stephan, Demetri, and Vlad advanced on Eldrick. Their combined electrical force pushed in on the stream from The Source until it shrunk back on him. When the warriors' energy touched Eldrick, he staggered back then fell into a crouch.

With a thrust of his thighs, he rose into the air. The three warriors followed. Stephan grabbed him from behind and placed an arm around his neck in a chokehold. Eldrick reached back, grabbed Stephan, and flipped him over his head. He flung the warrior to earth with enough force the ground rocked when he hit it.

Eldrick spun sideways. His legs cartwheeled out toward Vlad and Demetri. Luckily, the warriors moved in time to avoid the legs. Eldrick stopped upright between them and threw his arms out. The punches landed on their marks and snapped both heads back.

Eldrick brought both knees to his chest and kicked off Demetri. Looking like a swimmer doing the backstroke, Eldrick glided through the night air. When he came to a tree, he flipped and used the trunk to propel him forward toward the pair.

Vlad and Demetri broke away, heading for the ground.

Alex rolled onto all fours and used the timber he'd been leaning against to help him stand. Blazing pain burned through his body, but he pulled the tree up by the roots. He swung like a pinch hitter and caught Eldrick squarely in the stomach. The breath left his lungs in a hard puff as The Source tumbled ass over teakettle for the tree with Varrick's sword embedded in it.

Demetri beat him there and snapped the handle from the sword. The Alpha stepped aside a second before Eldrick's body fell on the weapon. Moonlight glinted off the blade where it protruded from his heart.

Eldrick slumped, blood rushing from the wound.

"Finally," Vlad whispered in a breathy voice.

"Tatiana!" Demetri ran to his mate and cradled her in his arms.

Her eyes fluttered open. "I'll be fine."

"Oh, thank the Fates!" Demetri hugged her tight.

Movement drew Alex's attention from the couple. Eldrick's hand twitched. Next, his leg moved. Surely, those were just death spasms.

The Source's head rose, and his eyes snapped open.

"Shit!" Alex yelled and backed from the tree.

A red aura glowed around The Source. Heat came from his body in powerful waves.

"Guys?" Alex called.

Nicholai rose. His chest still concave, it barely moved with each breath. "I know what to do. I know what the prophecy meant."

The Russian warrior looked at Demetri as if he was communicating over their mindlink.

"No!" cried Demetri. "There must be another way."

Nicholai gave him a sad smile and dissolved into a fine mist that headed for Eldrick. It disappeared when it approached.

Demetri stood. He, together with Vlad, approached Alex.

"When I give the order, we are to blast Eldrick with the demon fire."

Varrick and Stephan each powered up, no questions asked, from where they sat nursing their wounds. Desmond rose from attending to Marcus and did the same.

Alex turned toward Demetri. "Where'd Nicholai go?"

"Alex, focus. Build the energy." Demetri commanded then addressed the group. "Everyone, gather as much energy as you can and wait for my signal."

The warriors held their hands open in front of them and let the white energy coalesce in their palms. Even Marcus used the hand not holding his guts to form a ball. The combined energy built to an intensity so great it turned night into day, and Alex needed to close his eyes to the brightness.

"Hold," Demetri ordered. "Hooold."

"I don't know how much longer I can contain it," Vlad screamed over the deafening sound of the electric hum.

"Now!" Demetri yelled.

The Alphas hurled the energy toward Eldrick. He screamed. The smell of burnt flesh and hair assaulted Alex's nose.

The group let out a collective scream of agony. Alex bowed as excruciating pain seared through his body, burning white-hot. Alex's face contorted. It seemed as if his soul had been ripped from his body. This must be what it was like to experience one's sire dying, he reasoned. If the demons were right, Eldrick was the original vampire, so in a way, he'd sired them all.

Fates help them, the agony of his death hurt worse

than any of the physical injuries. After several long moments, the pain subsided. The group's groaning lessened. Alex used the respite to glance around. They were bruised, battered, but alive.

Demetri sank to his knees.

Nothing remained of the blade or The Source but a black outline in the shape of his body against the tree. In the middle, a white spot lay directly where his heart had been.

Tatianna crawled to the warriors. Demetri pulled her into his arms.

Tears flowed down her face. "I'm so sorry, Demetri."

"Sorry for what?" Alex asked, "We got him."

"Thanks to Nicholai," Vlad chimed in.

Alex glanced around. "Where is Nicholai?"

Concern tightened his gut.

"He's gone," Demetri answered in a tiny voice.

"What?" Vlad exclaimed.

When tears choked Demetri's reply, Tatiana explained. "Nicholai figured out the prophecy meant we needed to stop Eldrick's heart for the demonic electricity to fry him. He sent Demetri a plan over their mindlink so Eldrick wouldn't hear it. Nicholai became nothing more than molecules, went into Eldrick's body and wrapped around his heart. Once he stopped it from beating, he sent Demetri a signal to fry the bastard."

"Damn." Alex swayed on his feet.

Grief set in. He'd never see his friend again. He'd never laugh with Nicholai or hear one of those messed up colloquialisms he always used. Shock took his legs, and he fell to his knees.

The energy used to build that kind of electricity

combined with his grief and injuries to zap what little strength remained. Fatigue overcame him. He slumped forward. Pain roared through his body. Maybe he better lay down for a minute.

As Alex rested his head on the earth, blackness came to take the pain away.

****

Shira looked at her watch for the hundredth time since the warriors left. Where were they? How were they? How was Alex?

Worry tightened her stomach. She went to the door and opened it, knowing she'd see the same scene she'd seen each previous time this evening.

She glanced out on the empty drive. Her heart sank when there were no black SUVs waiting there.

Shira closed the door and turned to discover Harleigh behind her.

"Looking for Alex?"

Shira nodded. "Yes. I suppose you are here to check on Desmond."

When Harleigh nodded, her blue hair brushed her face. "Yep."

"As soon as Varrick returns, I plan on asking him for permission to take Desmond as my mate."

Shira's eyes widened. "Wow! That's great. I'm happy for you."

"Don't be happy yet. Let's see if Varrick allows it. Even if he does, we still have Stephan's approval to get as well."

Shira hugged Harleigh. "I'm sure it will work out."

Katrina rushed to the door.

"What's wrong?" Shira released the hug.

"Stephan contacted me. They are on their way

back. It was bad. Really bad. They need medical attention and…" she glanced between each of the demons. "someone didn't make it."

"Who?" Harleigh and Shira asked simultaneously.

Panic gripped her with its icy tentacles. Alex *must* be all right. She loved him. She hadn't been willing to admit it until right now, but she loved him. And faced with the idea of losing him, she realized she'd love him since the night at Cool Town.

Before Kat could answer their question, Christina rushed to the door and flung it open wide as the SUVs pulled up the drive. They came to a screeching halt, spitting gravel. Shira's trepidation increased when the leader of the Alphas jumped from the passenger seat looking like he'd aged twenty years over night. When Stephan opened the back door of the vehicle, she immediately recognized the booted foot hanging limply out the opening. It was Alex, and he wasn't moving.

Shira ran for the car, tears blurring her vision.

## Chapter 18

Shira's heart soared when Alex stirred under the blankets of the bed. His eyes opened and locked with hers. The aquamarine depths swallowed her whole, and she welcomed the sensation.

"You're awake."

Alex smiled, and the power of his dimple made her return the grin. "Worried about me?"

Shira scooted forward in her chair and took his hand in hers. The warmth soaked through her skin and assured her he'd be all right.

"Absolutely, Alex. You gave us all a terrible fright."

"I feel pretty good. How do I look?" He wagged his eyebrows, and Shira laughed.

"I can't believe you are fishing for a compliment."

"Always. I need constant reassurance my heartmate cares for me?"

"Heartmate? What's that?"

His face grew serious. "It means you are the other half of my soul. The Fates made us for one another. I can't live without you."

So, he felt as strongly toward her as she did toward him. The moment he'd returned to the plantation last evening, bruised and battered, she'd known. The brief time she thought he might have died nearly ended her. If there was any doubt of the depth of her feelings, last night erased them. The relief when he'd heal had been palpable.

"We have a similar concept. When demons find their mates, their bodies crave their mate's touch. It's as if the two of them truly become one. When they are apart, it's like half of them is missing."

Since they'd met, Shira's craving for the vampire had increased steadily. Though she didn't want to admit it at first, touching him made her complete and whole. She'd never been so connected to another person. Like an addict, her body craved Alex, needed his touch often to ease the burning pain of separation.

She brushed her fingers through his soft hair. "I like the word heartmate. It explains it nicely."

Alex cupped her cheek in his large hand. "The minute I drank your blood, I knew. You are mine, Shira. We are meant to be together."

Her heart sang. The smile that took her face reached her eyes. "I know. I feel it too."

Alex's arm dropped to the mattress. "I'm starving."

Shira jumped up and raced to the end of the bed. She pulled a glass of blood from the tray sitting on the white bench and brought it to Alex.

"Here. Stephan said you'd be hungry."

Alex propped himself up on one elbow and took the glass. When he finished, he handed the empty glass back to her then laid down.

"How are Stephan and the others?"

"Stephan seems fine. He has been healing the others as best he can. They are doing okay…physically."

Grief pulled the corners of Alex's mouth down. "None of us will be the same without Nicholai. He was a great guy. A superb fighter. I suppose you heard what happened?"

Shira nodded. "I'm so sorry about your friend. Demons have a saying; the essence of heroism is to die so others may live."

"I like that. Nicholai is a hero."

Shira placed her hand over Alex's heart. "As long as you keep him in your heart, he'll be with you always."

"He'd want us to be happy. In fact, I bet he's in the Great Beyond with Juliette right now, having a blast."

Shira chuckled. "I'm sure you're right."

Alex pushed into a seated position, and Shira leapt to adjust the pillow behind his back. The movement brought her head close to his. His masculine scent surrounded her, and she took a deep breath. When her breast touched his chest, a tingle went through her.

His breath ghosted over her cheek. Aware he stared at her, she turned her head in his direction. Her gaze dropped to his full lips then returned to his beautiful eyes. She swallowed her lust and straightened. As she moved to return to her seat, Alex grasped her wrist with a firm grip.

"Where do you think you are going?"

"I'm going to sit down."

Alex patted the bed. "Sit beside me."

Shira tucked her short skirt beneath her and did as instructed. The mattress sank under her slight weight, causing Alex to shift so their thighs touched. Something akin to electric current passed between them. A shiver went through her.

"You felt it too?" Alex asked.

Shira nodded.

The warrior pulled her into his arms.

Shira snuggled against her vampire. She must admit her body always felt right when it was with his. Now that her brain was on board with her body, she realized she'd always known they belonged together. She might have fought the idea, but she had always known deep inside.

Shira's heart jumped into her throat as she realized he'd been winning her heart piece by piece since his first cocky flirt. Like a drug addict needing a fix, she craved him with a physical, burning need.

Desire prickled over her skin.

"I can scent your arousal." Alex's whisky voice resonated in his chest.

Shira lifted her head. "You're recovering."

"I'm recovered enough."

Warmth flooded her core. "Are you sure? I don't want you to hurt yourself."

Alex gave her a cocky grin, flashing his dimple. "I'll show you just how sure I am."

He took her by the shoulders and pulled her into a passionate kiss that made her toes curl.

Shira heard a soft rumbling growl and realized the low, seductive sound came from the man before her. His arousal changed his scent. It became rich, musky and darkly spiced. She pulled away from his mouth to burrow her face in his neck, taking it deep into her lungs. Her tongue licked along his chorded nape and instinct made her bite.

She marked him as her mate. A tiny bit of his blood spilled from the wound. It set her core on fire as it traveled down her throat. More, she needed more. A shudder raced through his body, matching the one going through hers.

"You're mine," she whispered against his neck before she went in for another drink.

When the wound healed under her tongue, Shira pushed away from him, reached for his shirt with both hands and ripped the PJ open. She ran her hand slowly over his smooth skin, tracing the deep lines of his muscles. Starting with his shoulders, she worked her way down. Her fingers glided over his nipples and gave them a little pinch that made his hips buck before they traced the deep lines in his abdomen. Alex trembled, his muscles involuntarily jerking as she trailed the pads of her delicate hands over his body. She moved slowly, memorized the sensation of him.

His hand cupped her breast. He kneaded the flesh while he appreciatively eyed the voluptuous mound.

"Say it, again," Alex commanded in a low, sexy voice.

Shira's senses roared. Her fingernails lengthened slightly, reflexively, and she felt the bristling of the fine hairs on her arms. The animal within remained close to the surface, roaring for its mate in the recesses of her mind. The man laying before her, this glorious male with his impossibly sinuous body, belonged to her.

"You're mine," she purred from deep within her soul.

Shira kept her eyes locked with his as she moved the white comforter from his body. Anticipation lit his eyes, and she gloried in her ability to shake his usual calm. He guided her head to his most manly part. There was something exhilarating and intensely sensuous about the way the muscles in his jaw tightened, the way the deep rumbling in his chest reverberated as he fought to maintain some control of his body.

Shira took her time removing his pajama bottoms and underwear. The second his legs were free, his hands snaked into her platinum hair and fisted there. Shira wrapped a hand around his thick cock and stroked it with a slow rhythm. Alex let go with one hand and rested the arm behind his head. The other hand encouraged her to get on with business.

They didn't break eye contact as she took him into her mouth in one quick long thrust. He shivered slightly when she drew him out in a long slow pull. Her mate watched her tongue dart out to swirl around the tip of his hard shaft, once, twice, before licking a trail down the length of him. Her tongue followed a vein back up to make another swirl around the top before she took him in to suckle.

Alex moaned. His eyes closed at the sensation. His hips bucked helplessly as she worked him. Shira's hand wrapped around the thick base and began to stroke in time to the drawls of her mouth. The delicious sensation solicited a growl of approval from his throat.

Alex held out as long as possible, apparently drowning in the warmth of her mouth until he bit out from between clenched teeth, "I need to be inside you."

His hands swept through her hair, fingers curving until his nails ran over the sensitive skin on the back of her neck, erotically promising a night of ecstasy. Another gush of wet heat flooded her core.

"Shira." Her name rumbled coarsely from his throat.

His voice sent a shudder through her. She had pushed too far, sent him over the edge, and now she would reap the rewards of doing so. The mating would not be gentle but instead an animalistic taking.

Exactly what she wanted.

Alex grabbed her roughly by the shoulders and in a burst of preternatural speed removed the clothes from her body. He paused for a moment. His eyes burned a brand over her body.

"You're truly beautiful. Perfect in every way. I love you, Shira."

"I love you too, bloodsucker." Shira winked.

One eyebrow rose at the term, and that cocky grin returned showing his dimple.

"I suck more than just blood," he promised with a look that said he could eat her up.

Alex turned her and pushed her up onto her hands and knees on the bed. He moved behind her immediately and coiled a powerful forearm around her waist. His cock touched her entrance and anticipation made her whimper. He jerked her back, sheathing himself to the hilt in one long hard thrust.

Shira cried out, a gasp of carnal awareness and shock. Her body, eager and welcoming, became more aroused with each erotic rub as he burrowed against her. His heady smell mingled with her own, a delicious combination of male and female sex.

Alex's muscular arm wrapped around her like a band of steel across her hips, slammed her back against his hard maleness. His other hand braced his powerful body as it worked against her delicate opening. He pistoned into her, seating himself deep within on each stroke. Shira's passion built. Fire raced through her blood. Sweat dotted her forehead from their effort.

Pressure mounted within. It began in her tummy, moving outward until he took her over the precipice.

Shira screamed his name with the release, the sound echoing in the room.

As her inner muscles spasmed around him, he blanketed her body, forcing her shoulders to the bed while her hips remained high. His ragged breaths puffed against her back. She gazed at him over her shoulder, his eyes wanton. He took her mouth in a hard, possessive kiss that branded her as his. When she tried to turn away, Alex kept her there, demanding she comply with his desires.

His hand left her hip, sliding over her stomach to find the swaying mound of her breast. He cupped it and gave it a squeeze. Next, he took the nipple between his finger and thumb and twisted. It puckered eagerly under his ministration. The slight pain added to her pleasure. Shira moaned, pushed her bottom back against his hips, urging him to move.

Their bodies hammered together in a slapping of slick flesh as their tongues slid back and forth between their mouths. He tasted hot and spicy, tasted of sex. Shira broke the kiss while insistent thrusts rocked her. Alex's body demanded her compliance. Dominant and submissive, male and female, vampire and demon, an arousing example of opposites.

Urgency spurred each thrust. Shira belonged to him, and he made sure she knew it. She glanced over her shoulder in time to witness Alex bare his teeth. Fangs lengthened just before he pinned her to the bed. He bit into her creamy skin, hard enough to draw blood. The sucking at her neck timed perfectly with his thrusts. The erotic sensation sent her over the edge once more, expectant goose pimples bubbling up over her flesh. Their voices joined together in an exhilarating mix of animalistic growls and low moans when he joined her over the precipice.

After he pumped the last of his seed into her, she flattened out on the bed. Alex moved beside her and pulled her into his arms. She'd never experienced such love, physically or emotionally. A quiet peace overtook her, and she pillowed her cheek on Alex's chest. A finger lazily trailed over his pale flesh.

"Wow," Shira stated.

Alex's chuckle sounded in her ear. "I agree. I'd like to spend a lifetime doing that."

"Me too. Luckily, we'll have a long time to do just that since your blood can heal me if I get sick."

Alex gave her a squeeze. "I can't wait."

"Of course, we'll need to get Varrick's approval, but I'm sure he'll give it."

"Why do we need his approval?"

Shira pushed up on his chest. "Because he's my king. Besides I've already laid the groundwork. Harleigh and I have arranged a meeting to discuss the matter."

Shira glanced at the clock on the bedside table. "In fact, we are late."

Shira rose from the bed and began dressing.

"I'll never let you go, Shira." Alex's jaw flexed.

Shira crossed the room and patted his chest. "We'll figure it out. I'm sure he'll approve."

"He better." Alex rose from the bed and crossed his thick arms over his chest. "Because, if Varrick doesn't approve, he can go to Hell."

****

Thoughts of Nicholai pressed in on Alex as he and Shira walked down the hall. Only grief could temper the joy of finding his mate.

Just a short time ago, Alex envied Nicholai because the Alpha had finally found his mate, but the Fates had been so cruel. To take Julie after Nicholai had waited so damned long to find her…well, at least they were together now in the Great Beyond.

Tears threatened to form in his eyes, but he fought them back. Nicholai wouldn't want him grieving. If the warrior were here right now, Alex would bet every last penny that Nicholai would tell him not to waste a second of precious time with his heartmate. He'd no doubt say the best way to honor those lost was by living a joyful life with the woman he loved. And to do that, he just needed to take care of one little detail.

As they reached the bottom of the stairs, Alex gave Shira's hand a reassuring squeeze. She flashed him a gorgeous smile. Love sparkled in her red eyes.

"Ready?" Alex asked.

She nodded.

Alex and Shira entered the living room hand in hand. Desmond and Harleigh sat on one of Marcus' couches while Varrick and Stephan stood at the fireplace.

"Good evening," Stephan greeted. "Glad you could join us."

"Sorry we took so long," Alex offered as they made their way to the couch opposite from the other couple.

Harleigh flipped her pink bangs over her purple hair. "We were just discussing our situation."

"The way I see it, there isn't a situation," Alex challenged. "If a demon wants to mate with a vampire, then no one can stop them."

"I agree." Shira wrapped a hand around his bicep in a show of solidarity Alex appreciated.

No one was going to tell him he couldn't be with his heartmate. If it took leaving both the vampire and demon communities behind, he'd do it.

Varrick raised a meaty arm and held out his hand. "Don't get your hackles up, vampire. Stephan and I have already discussed the situation, and we've come to some decisions."

"We don't bloody well care what you decided," Desmond chimed in. "It's our lives, and we'll live them as we see fit."

Stephan lowered his head in a show of respect. "Just let us tell you what we are thinking."

Desmond's hand shot out in front of him palm up as if to say *go ahead.*

"We know how helpful it was for us to exchange blood before the battle," Varrick stated. "It gave us immense power and aided in defeating our enemy."

Stephan shifted his weight onto one leg. "We also know our blood can heal demons, which is a good thing. Once the demons no longer need to worry about getting ill, they will be able to live long, healthy lives. Therefore, we agreed that Varrick will keep a small supply of vampire blood for medical emergencies, and we will keep demon blood for battle purposes."

Varrick nodded. "However, it is too dangerous for all vampires and demons to have the powers Eldrick possessed, so we decided we won't exchange blood freely, only for the purposes Stephan mentioned."

Anger flashed over Alex's face, heating his cheeks. "Are you suggesting we don't exchange blood with our heartmates?"

Stephan straightened. "We want you to keep it to a minimum, and when you do, don't go around showboating your extra powers."

"You want us to hide?" Harleigh asked.

Varrick clasped his hands behind his back. "What we want is for you to keep the blood exchange in the bedroom, behind closed doors."

Alex smiled. "Well, that's doable. I've been wanting to try out the extra powers in the bedroom, anyway."

"You've got to try levitation sex. It's bloody brilliant." A mischievous expression took Desmond's face.

Harleigh gave Desmond a friendly swat on the shoulder. "Don't give him any ideas."

Shira laughed. "Oh, we have *got* to give that a try."

Alex rather liked that idea, and they better hurry before their blood exchange from earlier wore off.

Alex locked eyes with Stephan. "So, we're cool. Shira and I can be together. We just have to keep the monkey business in the bedroom."

Stephan nodded. "I would never stop you from being with your mate. I know how special a heartmate is."

Varrick nodded. "As do I."

Harleigh squealed with delight. "Thank you, Varrick. I knew you'd come around."

Joy spread through Alex's chest. He had everything he wanted, a beautiful, sexy heartmate who got his body humming like a finely tuned sports car *and* permission to exchange blood with her. Now all they needed was to decide where they'd live happily ever after, but that could wait. They had plenty of time to figure out the details, and Alex had no doubt everything would work out just fine.

Alex stood. “So, we are good then? We can go?”

Shira gave him an inquisitive look. “Where are we going to go?”

Alex flashed her a smile. “Upstairs. We have some levitating to do.”

He hoisted Shira over his shoulder and headed for the stairs, his heartmate’s throaty giggle racing straight to his groin.

## Epilogue

Julie and Nicholai floated through the Great Beyond toward the barrier between worlds, knowing that on every holiday, the barrier would be thin enough to pass through.

A thought took them to Marcus' home. They ghosted through the oak doors and into the foyer. A massive Christmas tree greeted them just as it had the previous ten years.

As her white gossamer gown settled around her body, Nicholai gazed down on his heartmate. Her radiant smile lit the room and made his heart sing.

Multicolored lights from the tree danced on the walls as the tree rotated in its base. The ornaments of all sizes, from tiny trinkets to globes the size of basketballs, glistened from the glitter and lights.

Desmond and Harleigh emerged from the living room.

"Deimos," Harleigh yelled. "Get down from there."

"Yes, Mummy," the dark-haired boy said before he straddled the banister and started down.

Desmond ran with blurring speed and intercepted his son seconds before he would have taken out the greenery wrapped around the banister.

The Alpha wagged his finger. "You know better than that. You're grounded."

Desmond placed the boy on the stairs and

proceeded down with him.

Harleigh pulled her red and green hair back in a ponytail and fastened it with a clip. “How about we postpone the punishment until tomorrow? It is Christmas after all.”

Desmond crossed his arms over his chest. “Maybe Santa will have something to say about that little stunt.”

Deimos’ eyes widened in horror. “I forgot Santa is coming tonight.”

Christina tsked as she entered the foyer from the opening to the parlor. “It would be a shame if he didn’t leave you any presents because you’d been naughty and broke Aunt Christina’s decorations. Lucky for you, your daddy caught you in time.”

Marcus chuckled as he joined the group and hooked an arm around his heartmate. “I think the poor boy has learned his lesson. You don’t have to threaten him with Santa.”

Juliette grasped Nicholai’s forearm through the white silk dress shirt he wore. “I wonder who is playing Santa this year.”

Nicholai shrugged. “I don’t know. I can’t imagine anyone topping Demetri playing him last year.”

Julie clapped her hands. “Oh, last year was fun. His little one recognized him immediately and ran into his arms.”

Her infectious joy made Nicholai chuckle before he wrapped an arm around Juliette’s shoulders. “I’m glad we come back every Christmas to check on them.”

“Me too. I hope the Council will continue these yearly get-togethers. I was afraid they’d never celebrate Christmas again once we died.”

“Me too. But then the children came.”

"That's such a miracle. Who would have thought the demon blood would fix the vampire infertility problem?"

Identical triplets with long, black hair ran down the hall, Viktor hot on their heels holding a slimy turkey bone in one hand. The girls screamed.

"Stop torturing your sisters," Natasha called from the kitchen. "Santa is watching."

"Humph, Santa doesn't scare me," Viktor declared.

Stephan caught the ten-year-old around his waist. When the child looked up, his bangs slid across his forehead. "You shouldn't say things like that. It will upset Analise, Anjelica, and Arianna."

Viktor settled. "I'm sorry. I know I should be nice to my sisters, but the triple A's get on my nerves."

Stephan nodded. "That's what sisters do, but try to be a little understanding. It's Christmas Eve after all. Now, why don't you help me get all the kids into the living room? I think I heard sleigh bells."

Viktor's eyes widened with excitement. "Really?"

He took off at a fast clip.

Katrina descended the stairs and wrapped an arm around Stephan's waist. "Where is our son?"

"Jaxson is in the media room with Marcus' spawn."

Marcus and Christina moved around the tree. Marcus huffed. "I heard that."

"What? It's true. Jax is down with Andres playing the latest zombie game. Honestly, Marcus, I think your child is a bad influence on mine," Stephan teased.

"Like father, like son," Kat quipped.

"Hey, I resemble that remark," Marcus agreed, and everyone shared a chuckle at the good-natured ribbing.

"Actually, Andres is a good boy," assured Tatiana. "He and Jaxson will make good additions to the Alphas, as will my Jay."

"Jayden will not be on the Council," Demetri announced, coming up behind Tatiana.

Nicholai wrapped an arm around Juliette's waist. "Jayden reminds me so very much of Natasha. Same black hair and silly grin."

Julie nodded. "But she has Tatiana's eyes."

Tatiana rounded on Demetri. "Jay can fight as well as any of the boys. There is no reason why she can't be on the Council."

Demetri's face reddened, and Nicholai didn't miss the telltale sign of his jaw tightening.

"Perhaps you two should discuss this later," offered Natasha. "Santa's ready."

His sister looked ravishing in a red dress with white faux fur accents. Motherhood agreed with her.

"Just in time, the kids are in the library."

The grownups moved into the library with Nicholai and Juliette hovering behind them. Christina had decorated the room like a winter wonderland. Paper snowflakes hung from the ceiling at various heights. White garland adorned the ladder on the bookshelves. The mantel over the fireplace hosted white candles in various sizes nestled in frosted greenery.

"Christina really outdid herself this year," Juliette breathed.

Nicholai took her hand in his. "I agree. It's almost as lovely as the time we went skating on the pond."

"Oh, that was such a wonder—" The sound of jingle bells in the fireplace cut off the remainder of Julie's sentence.

Santa materialized from within. The children stood and cheered his arrival. The grownups tried very hard not to laugh.

Juliette and Nicholai, however, laughed heartily knowing they couldn't be heard.

Julie covered her mouth with her hand. "Oh my gosh, it's Vlad."

The stoic Alpha, who never said much, was dressed in the traditional garb, complete with a white beard that didn't quite cover his black goatee. He scratched his head through the red hat.

"I bet that wig makes his head itch," Julie eked out between laughs.

Nicholai roared. "I never thought I'd see my brother-in-law in a Santa suit. I wonder how they ever convinced him to do that."

As if she heard him, Tasha murmured to Shira behind her hand, "I had to promise him a very special Christmas night to get him to agree to that."

"I bet." Shira bounced the baby in her arms.

Alex moved beside her and rubbed their son's white-blond hair. "At least the kids are loving it. Look."

Vlad sat in one of the wingback chairs, and the children all gathered round his feet.

"Ho, ho, ho," he bellowed in a deep voice. "Have you been good little vampires and demons this year?"

Cheers of "I have, I have" sounded in stereo with "yes" and "Uh-huh."

Santa Vlad laughed and shook his stuffed belly. "Well then, let's see what I have in my bag."

Andres and Jayden in unison cried, "PRESENTS!"

Everyone chuckled, no longer able to contain the joy of the moment.

"All of this is making me miss my girls," Julie said. "Let's go back into the Great Beyond and celebrate Christmas with them."

Nicholai leaned down and gave her a kiss. "Of course, *lastochka*, your wish is my commando."

Julie giggled. "I think you mean my wish is your command."

Nicholai affected a pleased expression. "That too. Now come. You know what to do. Just imagine the perfect Christmas in your mind, and it will be waiting for us when we get back to the twins in the Great Beyond."

"I'm so happy, Nicholai. You, me, and my daughters together for eternity, and we can come back to check on our friends and family whenever the veil between worlds is thin. This is heaven."

"Just being with you is heaven for me."

Love sparkled in Julie's eyes. "Who knew the afterlife would be this wonderful?"

Nicholai pulled Juliette into a loving embrace and smiled. Warm, white light filled their vision and as the couple faded back into the Great Beyond Nicholai whispered, "Sometimes the end is just a beginning."

**A word about the author…**

Born in Virginia, Brenda Sparks now resides in the Sunshine State. Balancing her writing with her personal life is challenging at times, but writing suspenseful paranormal romance is a passion that won't be denied. Her idea of a perfect day is one spent in front of a computer with a hot cup of coffee, her fingers flying over the keys to send her characters off on their latest adventure.

Brenda loves to connect with readers. Please visit her online and stop by her website to say hi.
http://www.brenda-sparks.com

Thank you for purchasing
this publication of The Wild Rose Press, Inc.

For questions or more information
contact us at
info@thewildrosepress.com.

The Wild Rose Press, Inc.
www.thewildrosepress.com

www.ingramcontent.com/pod-product-compliance
Lightning Source LLC
LaVergne TN
LVHW050629100826
845148LV00011B/1788

* 9 7 8 1 5 0 9 2 3 4 3 3 2 *